The right man, at the wrong time . . .

Although Alexis tried to fight it, she felt her cheeks heating up and knew that she was blushing. Massai noticed and gave her one of those dimpled smiles.

"What are you doing tomorrow afternoon before the concert? Why don't we get together and I can show you around New Orleans?" He took her response to his compliment to mean he could move forward.

"I don't think that would be such a good idea."

"And why not?"

"Because I just got out of a bad relationship, and I came to New Orleans to hear some good music and shop," gulping down her drink and feeling a little dizzy as a result.

"It's just a tour, not hot butt-naked sex. Anyway, I have a girlfriend." Taking another sip of his beer, he returned to watching the couples on the dance floor.

"If you have a girlfriend, why are you asking me out?"

"Because I was trying to be nice. You do know what that word means, don't you? I'm sure you do, even though you are showing me no evidence of such knowledge now. You know what? I think I'll leave you and your attitude alone. Have a *nice* evening." And with that, Massai grabbed his beer, and strolled over to the opposite side of the club. Alexis watched him retreat, feeling confused and alone and hoping she hadn't sworn off men too soon and would live to regret her words. Maybe she *had* been a tad too hasty.

WHERE I WANT TO BE

MARYAM DIAAB

Genesis Press, Inc.

INDIGO

An imprint of Genesis Press, Inc.
Publishing Company

Genesis Press, Inc.
P.O. Box 101
Columbus, MS 39703

All characters in this book have no existence outside the imagination of the author and have no relation whatsoever to anyone bearing the same name or names. They are not even distantly inspired by any individual known or unknown to the author and all incidents are pure invention.

ISBN: 13 DIGIT : 978-1-58571-268-7
ISBN: 10 DIGIT : 1-58571-268-X
Manufactured in the United States of America

First Edition

Visit us at www.genesis-press.com
or call at 1-888-Indigo-1-4-0

DEDICATION

To my mother, Diane Diaab and my grandmother, Gertrude Perry. Thank you for leading by example and teaching me that anything is possible.

ACKNOWLEDGMENTS

Wow! I can't believe the time has come for me to say thank you to everyone who has made this book possible.

First and foremost I would like to thank my husband, Damon, for his unwavering support, wonderful ideas, and constant patience. With you is where I want to be.

D.J. and Cameron, thank you for not bothering mommy too much when she needed to write.

To my father, Sabir Diaab, thank you for being my biggest fan.

Nancey Flowers, my agent, thank you for believing in my talent and finding this book a home.

To Deborah Schumaker, thank you for taking a chance on an unknown author and for answering my e-mails with kindness and patience.

And finally, to all the women who, from the beginning, loved Alexis and Massai as much as I do: Jamila, Nicole, Stacey, Tiffany, Mariam, Rahwa, Sharyl, Mornike, and Kelly. Without your input and advice there would be no *Where I Want To Be*.

1

WHAT'S GOIN' ON?

Alexis rolled over on her crisp, white Ralph Lauren sheets, an uncharacteristic splurge, and looked over at the pillow next to her. Kevin was gone. The man who had been there last night and gave her so much pleasure had disappeared—as usual. Her memories of their lovemaking vanished in an instant. She ran her manicured hand over the pillow, trying to gauge how long she had been sleeping alone. The cool pillow suggested she had probably been alone minutes after she had fallen asleep.

This disappearing act was an ongoing sore point between Kevin and Alexis in the six months they had been together. They would have amazing dates, followed by amazing nights together. Afterward they would talk about their hopes and dreams until they fell asleep in each other's arms. Alexis would wake up smiling until she saw and touched that cool pillow. She had questioned Kevin about it numerous times, and he always had what seemed to be a perfectly plausible excuse: He had to be at work really early in the morning, or he had to chauffeur his mother to the doctor. It was always something, and she always ended up frustrated and disappointed.

Alexis rolled out of bed, tugging at her white Victoria's Secret silk gown, which had bunched up around her waist, and crossed the carpeted bedroom to her beautifully decorated living room. Beige couches, matching chaise lounge, and antique walnut cocktail table, all purchased at estate sales and bargain warehouses, lent a warm and luxurious feel to the room. The walls had been recently changed from basic "apartment" white to a gorgeous shade of camel accented with midnight blue trim, reflecting Alexis's tastes and underlining her refusal to live in an apartment that was a clone of a hundred others. On the walls were black and white framed photos dating back to the late 1800s. The pictures had been passed down through her family for generations, and they explained her mixed heritage of African-American, Irish, and Spanish. That and her clear, caramel-hued skin, dark eyes, narrow nose and silky, naturally curly hair that when blown straight reached to the middle of her back.

In the kitchen Alexis noticed an expensive pair of gold hoop earrings lying on the breakfast bar and picked them up. She knew that Kevin had left them for her to soften the blow of waking up alone again. She gently slid each earring through her pierced lobes and thought of the man who had left them. Kevin was always doing sweet and thoughtful things like this, leaving little notes or gifts for her to find upon waking up. Alexis enjoyed such things, but she knew they were just attempts to mollify her mounting frustration. She would have much preferred to wake up in Kevin's arms instead of next to an empty pillow.

Kevin was everything that Alexis had always thought she wanted in a man. She had been instantly attracted to him when they met in, of all places, the grocery store. She clearly remembered the moment she saw the smooth-skinned, chocolate-brown man with the chiseled features, clean-shaven face and hazel eyes reading the back of a box of dryer sheets. He had taken her breath away, and she had nearly crashed her cart into the laundry detergent display. After getting to know him, Alexis found that, aside from being the most beautiful man she had ever seen, he was caring, sensitive, funny, an attentive lover and was a successful businessman as well. As the head of his own public-relations firm, he represented many of Detroit's most prominent figures and earned six figures a year. In addition, he was free to make his own work schedule. He wanted kids and even expected to be married some day. On paper, he sounded like the type of strong, independent and focused man that her mother, Dana, had always hoped and prayed her daughter would find. But in reality and in the cold light of day, there were problems with their relationship. Kevin's frequent disappearing acts were just the tip of the iceberg. They rarely went out and spent most of their time together eating takeout and watching DVDs in Alexis's apartment. When they did go out on a real date, it was somewhere so far outside of the city it was like being in another world. Kevin had never taken her to his home or to meet his parents, nor had he ever offered to.

Alexis knew all the signs were there, but she just didn't want to face them. She liked Kevin too much to believe, a la *Sex and the City*, that he "just wasn't that into her". Everything pointed to the obvious, but she believed the good outweighed the bad. He called daily, sent flowers often and when they were together it was as if they were the only two people on planet Earth.

Alexis sighed, flopped down on the couch and clutched a midnight blue and camel silk pillow to her stomach. Her conscience was trying to tell her that Kevin wasn't right for her, but her heart refused to listen. As always she wanted it to work and she wanted it to work right now. Ever since she was a little girl, she had wanted to have a lifelong love like that of her parents. Married thirty years, Dana and Isaiah Hunter met during their senior year of high school and had been together ever since. Their life had its ups and downs, its laughter and tears, but it was full and complete as long as they had each other. That's what Alexis yearned for, but thus far she had failed to make it happen.

Her history with men was not very encouraging, to say the least. It seemed as if the wrong men were drawn to her, and Alexis to them. She had dated the drug dealers, the women beaters; the ones with baby-mama dramas and the ones who couldn't, or wouldn't, keep their dicks in their pants. She had been used and abused so many times that when Kevin came along with all the right credentials and goals, she refused to see the problems that were so apparent to everyone else. After all, of the three children her mother and father shared, she was the only one who wasn't seriously attached. Her brother, Aaron, had married two weeks after she graduated from

college and her sister Alicia, though only a college sophomore, was planning her wedding for just a month and a
half away.

The ringing phone jerked Alexis back to reality. She
lifted the receiver off its base and, reading the caller ID,
smiled when she recognized the coming call from her
longtime best friend and confidant.

"What do you want?" Alexis asked Claire jokingly.

"Someone's in a funky mood this morning. Houdini
must have pulled another one of his little magic tricks,"
Claire laughed.

Alexis threw the pillow to the side and climbed off
the couch. Returning to the kitchen, she poured herself a
glass of orange juice. "Ha, ha, aren't you a regular Dave
Chappelle today. Are they giving you a show on Comedy
Central or will you stick to holding your sign off I-96?
'Will Tell Jokes For Food.' "

"Yeah, your attitude really is nasty today, so I know I
must be right."

"Look, I haven't got time to play your little games, so
let's cut this short. What did you call my house this early
in the morning for?" Finishing the orange juice, Alexis
rinsed the glass and placed it in the dishwasher.

"I called to tell you that everything is set for the trip.
We will be leaving on Thursday and the first concert
starts the next day. We reserved a room at the Ramada
Plaza right on Bourbon Street. We're not going—"

"What do you mean one room?" Alexis asked loudly,
cutting Claire off. "Three people are coming, right? And
I know how you can be. I am not going to have to sleep

in the lobby when you bring some local back to the room. No, I don't think so. I want my own room where I can have some rest and relaxation! I'm sure Morgan feels the same way with her overly-in-love ass." By now Alexis was checking herself in the bathroom mirror to make sure Kevin hadn't left any marks on her body as he had done the last time. She had made it a point of telling him that she was not a child and that if he wanted to mark his territory, he would have to do it by making a commitment, not by leaving tacky marks on her neck in the middle of summer.

"You're one to talk. Always making excuses for Kevin. Anyway, Ms. High and Mighty, all the hotel rooms are booked for that weekend, and if you can find something else in that area and for that price, *please* be my guest. Don't you think I would rather have my own room? All your granny-acting ass is going to do is cramp my style, anyway. Talking about getting some rest and relaxation in New Orleans! There is something seriously wrong with you. We are going to Crescent City, the Big Easy. We are not going to sleep; we are going to party and if you are going down there for any other reason than that, then you should stay home and knit."

Alexis laughed and remembered why Claire was her best friend. She had the balls to tell not just Alexis, but everyone, how she saw it and didn't care what someone thought afterward. She was honest, blunt and straight to the point. Alexis thought that every woman needed a Claire in her life.

"Anyway," Claire continued, "we are going down there to celebrate your birthday, so *you* of all people should be planning to have the time of your life. And again, *you* of all people should be trying to find a local to have a little fling with, considering what you have—or rather, don't have at home."

In that moment Alexis regretted ever telling Claire anything about Kevin and his highly suspect behavior. Claire reminded her of the fact that though Kevin had the means, he was often times less than attentive, and she was of the mind that he either had someone on the side or was on the downlow. Alexis personally thought Claire had been watching entirely too much *Oprah*.

"Okay, well, whatever you think is irrelevant to me right now. I am not that kind of girl, and I am going down to New Orleans to hear some great music, go sight-seeing, eat some awesome food and shop. Notice how I didn't include boning the first Southern guy that crosses my path on my itinerary," Alexis said matter-of-factly as she searched through her closet for her favorite fuchsia and white yoga outfit.

"Alexis, you are so stuck up that it's disgusting. Anyway, as I was saying before I was so rudely inter-rupted, we are not going to all the concerts because some of them just aren't that great unless you're a baby boomer. On Friday, they have Destiny's Child and Floetry on the main stage. Then they have Alicia Keys and John Legend. Sunday, Kanye West and Common will be performing. Since you are off work the entire summer we figured that we would stay an extra day and leave Tuesday morning."

That was what Alexis loved about teaching—all the time off. She looked forward to summer vacation and always used that time to do the things she hadn't the time to do during the school year. Traveling was one of those things. Thinking about the upcoming trip, Alexis couldn't help but smile. Leave it up to her girls, Claire and Morgan, to plan the trip to end all trips. She had always wanted to go back to New Orleans, and had fond memories of the time the three traveled down to the Big Easy for Mardi Gras during their junior year of college. That had been a trip they would never forget. The wild things that had happened there always put smiles on their faces but would have to remain there. *What happens in New Orleans stays in New Orleans.*

"Claire, this trip is going to be great. Thank you so much for planning it," Alexis said sincerely.

"No problem; that's what best friends are for. Just remember to keep your ass out of that hotel room and in the streets with Morgan and me and you will be fine." With that, Claire slammed down the phone in Alexis's ear, praying that her friend wouldn't ruin the trip she'd so painstakingly planned.

Returning home from the gym, Alexis felt relaxed and rejuvenated; yoga usually did that for her. Not only was it a good workout that kept her five foot, six inch, 125-pound frame toned, it also helped her to clear her mind and make her more focused. She needed this degree of focus to deal with Kevin, having decided to call him and find out what plans he had for the evening. She wanted to spend as much time with him as possible in the two and a half days before leaving for New Orleans, but more importantly, she wanted to find out what excuse he had for leaving her bed this time.

Alexis threw her gym bag onto the navy, camel and white checkered duvet cover and picked up the cordless phone from the glass end table next to her bed. She dialed Kevin's cell number, and he picked up after the fourth ring.

"Kevin Washington." Kevin's deep baritone voice did things to her body that no one else's had ever come close to. Just hearing it made her tingle, and she was instantly aroused.

"Hi, baby. How are you?" Alexis asked, trying to match the sexy timbre of his voice.

"I'm good. Busy. I'm sorry about this morning, but I had an early meeting and I didn't bring my suit over to your place last night. You know how my memory is."

"I know, I know. But it would be nice if we could spend just one *full* night together every once in a while." Alexis inserted a pout into her voice and hoped he heard the disappointment.

"It's coming, baby, I promise. But work has been so hectic these past few months. Trying to land this new account has left me little to no free time. As soon as all this madness is over, I'll take you anywhere you want to go. Paris, Spain, sky's the limit," Kevin said, trying to pacify Alexis yet again.

"I don't need all that, Kevin. I will be completely satisfied if you would just stay the entire night with me. I mean, we have been pretty serious for six months now and every time we make love, you take off like a thief in the night. I'm beginning to think that something is going on."

"Alexis, I can assure you that nothing is going on. As I said before, I'm just really swamped at work. Anyway, on a more pleasant note, I'll be over tonight around seven with your birthday present."

"Kevin, how many times do I have to tell you not to get me anything?" she asked firmly, even though she was already excited about the promised gift. Maybe it would match the earrings he'd left that morning.

"I can't help it. You are so wonderful, and it's the least I can do. I love to see you smile. I'll see you soon."

Alexis hit the end button on her phone and sighed. Kevin always knew exactly what to say to make her forget her anger and disappointment. But none of that really mattered because, right words or not, she still had that nagging feeling in the pit of her stomach that something was not quite right with their relationship.

2

MISSION IMPOSSIBLE

Alexis spent the hours before Kevin's arrival cleaning her apartment and beautifying herself, confident that once Kevin saw her and the romantic atmosphere she had created he would have no choice but to spend the *entire* night in her bed.

The ivory-colored candles on her coffee table gave the living room a softly radiant glow. Alexis pushed a button on the universal remote and the room filled with the sweet, jazzy sounds of Kem. The music flowing from the CD player in the walnut entertainment system produced the illusion of a live concert in Alexis's mind. Satisfied with what she had accomplished, she looked in the mirror to make sure she herself was nothing short of perfection. Her long, dark hair cascaded down her back in loose curls, and the royal blue lace baby doll she recently purchased from Victoria's Secret accentuated her curves wonderfully. She had made the right decision to forgo the matching thongs.

Alexis went into the kitchen to check on the lobster tails with drawn butter she was preparing for dinner. She had considered creating an elaborate dessert of chocolate-covered strawberries but had decided against it. She would be Kevin's dessert tonight. She returned to the living room and fluffed the couch pillows. This was the most anxious she had ever been. This was her night. This was the chance she had been waiting for to prove all the doubters and cynics wrong. She believed that Kevin was a good man, a hardworking man. If he couldn't spend every night with her, that was okay. *Really*. But tonight Alexis planned to put on a show so spectacular that if he left before sunrise then Claire was right, he really must be on the downlow.

She took one final look in the mirror and pulled her orange terrycloth robe over her lingerie to add a bit of mystery. Men always wanted what they couldn't have, and that was exactly the reaction she was going for. She wanted Kevin to want her. The guest of honor hit the brass doorknocker three times, and Alexis blew a kiss at her reflection and went to the door to let him in.

"Hey, baby. How are you?" Kevin asked, looking curiously at the almost frumpy robe covering Alexis's body. He bent to kiss her and tried to peek inside the robe.

"Will you stop that?" she said, playfully smacking Kevin's hand away from her robe. "You need to learn patience. I make the rules tonight. You will see what's under this when *I'm* good and ready, and not a second before." She took Kevin's black Coach briefcase from his hands and placed it on the floor beside the couch.

"So it's like that? You run the show? Well, what exactly are you running? And what's under that ugly-ass robe?"

"Number one, my robe is not ugly; it's comfortable. And number two, because *I* run the show, *I* make the rules, and you need to just follow along and enjoy the ride."

"So there will be riding involved?" Kevin asked, smiling slyly.

"Your problem is that you have a one-track dirty mind. I made dinner, and I want you to sit down here," Alexis commanded, pointing to the chaise lounge. Kevin smiled again and sat down as instructed.

Alexis went to the kitchen and bought out a platter of lobster tails and butter. She sat next to Kevin and tearing pieces of meat from the shell, and dipping them in the butter. She placed a succulent morsel into Kevin's mouth. "Tell me about your day."

Kevin looked at Alexis and sized up the situation. From the sensual aura of the apartment to the orange robe she kept tied, he could tell that tonight she meant business. She had a hidden agenda, and he knew it.

He chose his words carefully. "I had an eight a.m. meeting with the mayor today to discuss that little situation he's been trying to dodge. That lasted about two hours. Then I went back to the office to check on the employees, as well as on the status of that new jazz club account I've been telling you about. We're trying to plan its opening, and the owner is being really difficult. So I really have to stay on top of my staff to make sure they are giving the client what he wants, but are not getting run over in the process. After that, I went to lunch with a client at The Loving Spoonful, went back to the office and now I'm here."

Alexis put another bite of lobster tail into Kevin's mouth and licked the extra butter off her fingers slowly and enticingly. She smiled secretly when she saw the bulge inside his pants grow.

"And how was your day?" he asked, easing one hand up under the robe and caressing her bare thigh while the other hand moved to uncover what was under wraps. She swatted his hand away, but not before he glimpsed the swell of her bronzed cleavage, feeling his dick grow a little bit harder and a little bit longer.

"My day was okay." Alexis told Kevin about her conversation with Claire, her upcoming birthday trip down to New Orleans and her yoga workout.

"I hate that you're going to be gone for nearly an entire week. Why don't you stay here and let me do something special for you on your birthday?" he asked, now running both hands along Alexis's body through the thick fabric of the robe.

"Kevin, Claire and Morgan have been planning this trip for months, and I really want to go. We have tickets to the Rhythm and Blues Festival, and you know how great those concerts are. Besides, I'll only be gone for a few days, and you know what they say: 'Absence makes the heart grow fonder,' " Alexis cajoled, popping a bit of lobster tail into her own mouth.

Kevin kissed her neck, again attempting to look into her robe. Getting ever closer to his goal, he saw the vibrant blue lacy fabric and the way her breast nearly spilled out the top. At this point, his dick grew to maximum capacity, and it was taking all his willpower not to take off that robe and bury his face into Alexis's chest.

"Why are you doing this to me?" he asked, moaning and rubbing his dick through the smooth fabric of his pants.

"I'm not doing anything," Alexis responded innocently. "I'm just trying to give my man a delicious and relaxing dinner after a very hard day at work. Now is there anything wrong with that?"

"No, baby, of course not."

"Good. Now if my memory serves me correctly, you said that you have something special for me?"

"Yes, as a matter of fact, I do. It's in my briefcase." Kevin retrieved his briefcase from the floor and removed the robin's egg blue box that every woman loves to see. "Happy birthday."

Alexis looked at the long box in her hand and was fairly certain it contained a watch or bracelet. She smiled at Kevin and kissed him before opening the box. Alexis smiled delightedly as she lifted the platinum heart and key bracelet from the cotton cushioning. He took the gift from her hands and placed it around her wrist.

"Kevin, you are so sweet. I know that thank you is not enough, but thank you," Alexis gushed, looking down at the bracelet.

"Anything for you, Alexis. I've told you how I feel about you and our relationship. I want to take care of you and shower you with the finer things in life. This," he said, lightly touching the bracelet, "is just the beginning."

Feeling overwhelmed by his thoughtfulness and generosity, Alexis decided to stop playing games and show him just how much she appreciated his kindness. Placing the half-eaten platter of lobster on the coffee table, Alexis rose and looked at Kevin intently. Standing up, she slowly began to loosen the belt around the robe, watching Kevin's reaction as she let it fall from her shoulders into a heap around her stiletto-clad feet.

"Damn! Don't you look delicious?" Kevin asked, removing his jacket and tie as Alexis stood before him.

Hands on her shapely hips, she did a little twirl to give him the full effect. "I take it you like what you see?" she asked seductively.

"Like is definitely not the word for how I feel right now."

"And exactly what word would you use to describe what you're feeling right now?" she asked, kneeling in front of him and removing his belt.

"Lucky."

"Well, I'm glad, because all this," she said, running her hands down her body, "is for you." Alexis placed her right hand on Kevin's midsection and felt the bulge through the fabric of his pants. He let out a deep moan and began to explore under her lingerie. She involuntarily arched her back, bit her lower lip and felt her body start to tingle and throb from Kevin's touch.

"Damn, you feel so good," he said, looking Alexis in the eye as he rubbed his thumb along her nipple through her bra. Feeling the dampness between her legs, she grasped his free hand and guided it to the spot that always drove her absolutely wild. He gently caressed, stroked and prodded until she could take no more and begged for him to go inside her.

"I need you," was all she said before she bent over and removed his pants and boxer shorts in one fast motion. Straddling his lap, she grabbed Kevin's smooth dick, took a Trojan from the "candy" dish next to the couch, positioned it, and, without reservation, began to bounce on his dick as if it were a trampoline. The more she worked her body, the louder Kevin's moans became. When he pulled her bra straps from her shoulders and fixed his eyes on her bouncing thirty-four D breasts she knew that he was nearing climax. As Alexis felt Kevin's body begin to tense and tremble, she decided to try something she had read about but had never tried. She reached behind her and gently cupped Kevin's balls.

"Wh-what—what are you doing, girl? Wh-where did you learn—" Kevin was shaking and sweating so much he couldn't finish his sentence. She moved her body faster as her hand jiggled down below. "I'm not ready yet. This feels too good. Stop. Not yet."

Alexis smiled and felt truly powerful as Kevin filled the condom. A few hollers later, he rested his head on her shoulder. "Damn, girl, I'm never leaving your ass."

Mission accomplished.

3

WEDDING BELLS

Alexis was awakened by a loud crashing sound. She shot straight up and looked over on the dresser at the alarm clock. It was 6:05a.m.

"Why didn't you wake me up?" Kevin demanded, coming out of the bathroom and frantically pulling his pants over his boxer shorts.

Alexis rolled her eyes and lay back down, pulling the sheet over her head to hide the smile that had enveloped her face. "I didn't wake you up because you were sleeping. Waking you up would have been impolite. What's the big deal, anyway?"

"The big deal, Alexis," he began, a tinge of sarcasm in his voice, "is that I have an appointment this morning, and I don't have a change of clothes." As she watched in disbelief, he continued pulling on pieces of clothing. Today was Saturday. Kevin made it a point never to work on the weekend, and she knew this.

"You know what, Kevin? You are full of shit. Today is Saturday, for God's sake, and I *know* you don't work on Saturday or Sunday. If there is some *real* reason that you refuse to stay the night with me, then just tell me. I may be a couple years younger than you, but I'm a big girl.

Believe me, I can take it." Alexis jumped out of bed and challenged him face to face.

"Baby, there is absolutely nothing I have to tell you. No secrets. I am just going to be severely late for work if I don't leave within the next five minutes."

She looked at him, shaking her head helplessly. This man was impossible, and he was well on the way to making it that much easier to believe what Morgan and Claire kept telling her.

Hearing the phone ring, Alexis walked over to her bedside and angrily snatched it up. She was ready to give it to whoever had the gall to call her home this early on a weekend. "Hello?" she hollered into the phone, glaring at Kevin out of the corner of her eye. She needed to get this person off the phone before he tried to make his exit. They had a lot more talking to do.

The female voice on the other end sounded as if she was crying, and Alexis could barely understand her as she asked, "May I speak with my husband, Kevin Washington please?" Those nine words made Alexis feel as if she had been punched in the chest. All the air rushed from her lungs and she gasped loudly. She had heard the woman, not loudly or clearly, but she had definitely heard her. She had asked for her husband, Kevin Washington. *Her* Kevin Washington, or rather, the man she thought was hers.

"Pardon me?" Alexis said, her voice cracking, the lump in her throat causing it to constrict.

"My husband, Kevin Washington, is he there? The kids woke up this morning asking for him. He normally comes home, but he's been gone two nights in a row . . ." she sniffled. Alexis wondered how long the woman had been crying. "I've had your number for quite some time. You called his cellphone one day when he was in the shower and I wrote the number down. He often calls out your name in his sleep, so I knew you two must have been seeing each other."

Wait one damn minute! Did this woman just say kids? This jackass not only failed to let me know he had a wife but failed to let me know about children as well? And did she just say he hadn't been home in two nights?

"Two nights? He's only been here with me one." Alexis was both angry and addled.

"Well, this isn't the first time he's gone outside our marriage," his wife whispered. "How long have you been seeing him?"

Alexis sat down on the side of the bed feeling as if her legs were about to collapse. She looked around the bedroom for him and heard the jingle of his keys in the living room.

"We've only been seeing each other six months, but this explains a lot. I can't tell you how sorry I am for this whole situation. I had absolutely no idea. I mean, I am not the kind to date another woman's husband." She felt horrible and wanted to let the woman know that he had deceived her as well.

"Kevin, don't leave yet. There's something I really need to talk to you about. It'll only take a minute, and I promise you won't be late for your meeting. I just need to finish this phone call," she said, talking in the sweetest and sincerest voice she could manage under the circumstances.

"Can you please hurry up? I really need to get out of here!" he said, his frenzy growing, his normally deep voice rising a few octaves as Alexis entered the room with the phone still at her ear.

The woman heard Kevin's distinctive voice and began crying louder. "I'm sorry to call your house this early but my husband, the kids—I just don't know what to do. I love him."

"I had absolutely no idea. I was never told because if I had been this would not be happening, I assure you. I truly apologize to you for this misunderstanding," Alexis reiterated. The lump in her throat had disappeared, replaced by a steady pounding in her head.

"I figured you didn't know. I guess he's playing both of us."

Still holding the phone, she slowly walked over to the couch where Kevin was impatiently sitting and sat down next to him. "I guess so," was all that she could say to the woman, who was obviously and rightfully hurting a lot more than she was.

"May I speak with him, please?" his wife asked.

Without comment, she handed the phone over to a startled and confused Kevin. He looked at Alexis questioningly before hesitantly speaking into the phone. Upon hearing the voice at the other end, he refused to look at Alexis as she sat with her arms folded across her chest, feeling the heat of anger rising within her body.

"Okay, Kimberly. I know. I'm on my way," Kevin said quietly, hanging his head. Kevin pressed the end button and placed his hand on Alexis's knee.

"Don't touch me, Kevin!" she said with so much hate and anger she barely recognized her own voice.

"Come on, baby, let me explain."

When he reached to touch her knee again, Alexis jumped up off the couch and stared down at him. "I said don't touch me!" she screamed nearly at the top of her lungs. "Look, asshole, you don't have anything to explain to me. I can sum up this situation for the both of us. You are a liar and a cheater. You are selfish and self-centered. I honestly wish I would have never met you, and I want you out of my house. NOW!"

"You want me out of your house? Alexis, don't you think you're being a little overdramatic? You haven't even let me explain the situation," Kevin said, attempting to plead his case from the couch.

Alexis stood across from him with her hands on her hips. "Okay, Mr. Washington, let's hear it. What could you possibly say that is going to justify what you have done not only to me, but more importantly to your wife and children?"

He took several deep breaths before beginning what Alexis had already concluded would be another lie. "Well, Jessica and I have been married for about five years now. We got married right out of college and only did that because she was pregnant. After K.J. was born, we had another baby right away, a daughter named Mariah. I realized after her birth that I wasn't really in love with my wife, and the longer we were married, the further apart we drifted. Even though I adore my children, I have been unhappy in my marriage for a long time. When I met you and we started dating I finally began to feel happy again."

Alexis laughed bitterly. "Somebody give me a shovel, because right now I'm knee-deep in shit. Do you seriously think that being unhappy with your wife is any kind of excuse? You could have just divorced her instead of being so manipulative and deceitful. You made me believe that you wanted to get married and have kids, Kevin!" she yelled, becoming angrier by the minute. "Well, I guess that joke is on me because you're already married and you already have kids. And who the hell is Jessica? I could have sworn that you just called your wife Kimberly when you were talking to her on the phone!" she resisted the urge to lunge at him and scratch his eyes out.

Kevin looked like a man defeated and hung his head in either shame or self-pity; she couldn't tell which. He stood and took three steps towards her with his hand outstretched. "Okay, no more lies. Jessica is another woman that I've been seeing on and off for a couple months, but she can't compare to you. None of them can."

"So what you are telling me is that you are not only cheating on your wife but on me, too? You know what, Kevin? You are unbelievable. Out of all the men I have dated, never in my life have I been with someone as despicable as you."

"Don't be that way, Alexis, we can work this out. I am prepared to leave both of them for you. Let's talk about this."

She took a step back from him and laughed again. "Leave both of them for me? Are you listening to yourself? Fool me once, shame on you. Fool me twice, shame on me, and I am not a shame-on-me type of woman. And why should I be with you? Why should I when I know you'll just turn around and do the same thing to me after I stretch out my body to push out a couple of your kids? I can do bad all by myself."

"I love you, Alexis, don't you understand that? I want to make you my wife," Kevin begged, reaching for her hand. She immediately snatched it from his grasp and stepped further back.

"This is the last time I'm going to ask you to leave."

"You're making a mistake, and I don't plan to give up on us," Kevin promised, slowly picking up his briefcase and walking to the door.

"That's funny, Kevin, really comical. There is no US; however, there is you, your wife and your kids. Oh, and let me not forget, your girlfriend. And as far as I am concerned, the only mistake I made was getting involved with you."

4

ARE LESBIANS IN?

"Why didn't you call me back yesterday? Were you that damn busy?" Morgan asked, as she, Claire and Alexis flipped though the racks at Express, one of their favorite clothing stores. The trio had been shopping since the mall opened at 10 a.m., looking for outfits for their to New Orleans trip. Shopping trips like this were a ritual for them. The day before every trip they took together, they would shop until they dropped. They would follow up by pampering themselves with facials, manicures, pedicures and getting their hair styled at the salon where Morgan worked as head stylist. The three friends loved these outings because they allowed them to accomplish their two favorite things at once—bonding with each other and shopping.

"Why I didn't call you back is none of your concern," Alexis said, removing a sky blue tank top from a rack and holding it up to her chest. Alexis checked the price and size on the tag hanging from the shirt's hem.

"What in the hell is your problem? You have been acting really shitty all morning," Morgan asked, tossing a purple bikini top back onto the shelf and glaring at Alexis.

"Oh, I know what the problem is," Claire said, she too glaring. "You know Mr. Six Figures doesn't like to stay the night after he gets his rocks off. He probably up and left before *you* had a chance to visit with Big O."

Alexis returned the tank top to the rack and looked at her two best friends. "It's much worse than that."

Claire and Morgan looked quizzically at each other and then at Alexis. "What happened?" Morgan asked. The anger and annoyance previously in her voice disappeared and was replaced by empathy and concern.

"Well, the night before last—" Alexis began.

"Oh, my God, you caught him with another man, didn't you? I swear, that is just like something you would read in an E. Lynn Harris book. I knew he was on the downlow. I knew it! After I heard that man on *Oprah* explaining that kind of lifestyle I knew Kevin fit the profile."

"Why must you always be so dramatic?" Alexis asked impatiently. "Kevin Washington is not on the DL, at least not in the way you think."

Alexis saw the total confusion in her friend's eyes. "He's married," she said, looking from Claire to Morgan.

The two gasped simultaneously.

"Wait, I'm not finished. Not only is the man married but he has two kids."

Morgan clamped her hand over her mouth in shocked disbelief. "Oh, my Lord," she said quietly.

"Ain't that a bitch?" Claire asked, shaking her head. "Well, I knew *something* wasn't right with him. I would have never guessed that he was married, though."

"I know. I feel so completely clueless."

"Why?" Morgan asked. "It's not your fault. He's the one that lied to you," Morgan said, giving Alexis a sisterly hug.

Feeling a lump form in her throat and her eyes well with tears, Alexis unsuccessfully tried to keep her emotions in check. Tears began streaming down her face, prompting Morgan to hug her even tighter.

"Girl, stop crying over his low-life ass. You are better off without him as far as I'm concerned. He didn't do anything but piss you off with all that disappearing stuff, anyway. Not to mention the fact that you were beginning to question yourself—like something was wrong with you! But you probably will miss those gifts," Claire said, never failing to find the humor in a situation.

As much as Alexis didn't want to admit it, she knew Claire was right. Alexis stepped out of Morgan's hug and wiped her eyes. "Okay, you're right. I am better off without him." But Alexis thought that was easy to say but not that easy to make herself believe.

"I know I'm right. Now that you got your little crying jag out of the way, tell us how you found out."

Taking a deep, cleansing breath and standing up straight, Alexis began to tell her story. "Well, I called him to find out why he had left early again, and he gives me his usual excuse about needing to go to some early-morning meeting. Then he tells me that he's coming over later and that he has a present for me. I get all cute and light candles and I even prepared lobster." Alexis told the story in hushed tones so that the entire store wouldn't be privy to her life. "He gets there and we're talking. We sit on the chaise and I start feeding him lobster and he gives me this beautiful platinum heart and key bracelet. After that, you know I had to put it on him. My dumb ass thought he was being thoughtful and sweet. Anyway, we fall asleep, but he wakes up about six and is banging about, snatching on all these clothes and about to fall over, talking about he's going to be late for work. It's Saturday."

"Girl, you know he was a fool. He couldn't even get his lie straight enough to realize that it was the weekend," Claire interrupted.

"Oh, you haven't heard the worst of it. As he's panicking trying to get out of my apartment, the phone rings, and it's his wife telling me that he hasn't been home and his kids miss him. She asks to speak to him and I oblige."

"Are you serious?" Morgan asked, not wanting to believe what she was hearing.

"Girl, yes, I almost fell out. Anyway, after he gets off the phone with her, I tell him that he needs to get the hell out. He tries to explain, but then he calls his wife by the wrong name. And after all that I come to find out he's not only cheating on his wife with me but with some other chick, too." Alexis felt exhausted. Retelling that story was both physically and emotionally draining.

"This is the first time in my entire life that I have been absolutely speechless. I feel like I need a drink," Claire said, returning to her search through the racks.

"If you feel like having a drink, what do you think I feel like?"

"Probably like smoking some crack," Morgan said, following Claire over to the clearance section.

After each woman had spent nearly two weeks' pay on clothing and spa treatments, hunger set in and they ended their day with dinner at Angie's Soul Food Café.

"You know what, Alexis? You should just consider what happened between you and Kevin as a blessing in disguise. I mean, now that you are unattached, you can really let loose in New Orleans without worrying about what anyone else is going to say. You can even join in my quest for the sexiest Southern gentleman," Claire said, spearing one of Angie's famous salmon croquettes with her fork.

Alexis laughed. "The only thing this experience has taught me is that men are not to be trusted."

"Not all men are like that, Alexis. Look at Craig and me. We have been together for almost four years and are truly happy. He has never cheated on me, and it's going to stay that way," Morgan said wistfully, taking a sip of her mango-flavored iced tea.

Claire rolled her eyes, and Alexis reached across the table and placed her hand over Morgan's. "You honestly don't have a clue, do you?" Alexis asked, her tone mockingly soothing.

"What is that supposed to mean?" Morgan asked angrily.

"Nothing. Alexis is just throwing salt because her man turned out to have more women than Bishop Don Juan," Claire said.

Alexis gestured with her middle finger and continued. "All I'm saying is that I'm tired of being played and mistreated. My love life seems as if it's in a never-ending downward spiral. Last year, it was Michael with his controlling ass; the year before that it was Mama's Boy Quentin. Now Kevin. It just seems like all the men who are attracted to me and vice versa are completely incapable of showing me the love and respect I deserve. I refuse to put myself through that again, and I am okay with the fact that I'll be spending the rest of my life alone."

"You sound really ridiculous. You aren't even twenty-five yet, and you're already planning to be an old maid. I don't know why I'm your friend, because we have absolutely nothing in common. And when I spoke about the men in New Orleans, I wasn't suggesting you find a husband. I was suggesting you find someone to bang your brains out and make you forget all about Kevin. Or is he going by Hugh Heffner now?"

"Look, I am not going down there to get involved with any man on any level. I just want to forget about men totally and concentrate on other more productive and rewarding things."

"I just don't understand how you can say that because as long as we've known each other, which has been a very long time, you have been talking about wanting to get married and be a mother and do all the things that you need a man to accomplish," Morgan reminded Alexis.

She had to admit Morgan was right. When Alexis met Claire and Morgan the day she and her family moved into the neighborhood, all Alexis talked about was getting married and having five little girls. At just seven years old, she would devote hours to creating Barbie Doll wedding dresses out of her brother's sweat socks while other children her age were out riding their bikes or playing freeze tag. In high school, Alexis became a majorette just to be noticed by the most popular guy in school. And in college, she started a hope chest so that when the right man came along and asked her to marry him, she would be ready.

"I just have one question, Alexis," Morgan continued, putting down her fork and looking Alexis straight in the eye. "Are you planning on becoming a lesbian? Because that's what it sounds like to me."

"Good question," Claire concurred, turning in her seat to look at Alexis.

Alexis sighed, this time giving both of them the middle finger. "No, that is not what I'm saying. What I am saying is that no man is worth the pain and humiliation that I've had to deal with these past few years. I know it's sad and completely against the things I have always wanted for my life, but if I have to be celibate in order to protect my heart and save my sanity, then that's what I will do."

"Well, instead of this trip for your birthday, we should have gotten you a lifetime supply of batteries, because you are going to rack up a lot of miles on your vibrator."

5

THE BIG EASY

Alexis stepped onto the latticed balcony of the hotel room she was sharing with Claire and Morgan, and the suffocating Louisiana heat drove her straight back into the air-conditioned room.

"Why is it so hot out there? It feels as if we just touched down into the depths of hell," she said, closing the French doors behind her and sitting on the bed next to Morgan.

The three had arrived in New Orleans earlier that day after a three-hour flight and were completely excited to finally be there. The hotel room was gorgeous and had two double beds, a Jacuzzi tub, a minibar, and a separate sitting area. The walls were the color of a deep wine and exuded indulgence and sensuality, much like New Orleans itself. From the moment they arrived, Alexis and Morgan had raved about their accommodations, while Claire had proclaimed that the room was too nice for them not to be spending much time there. "Had I known it would be like this, I would have saved my money and reserved three separate rooms at the local motel near the airport," Claire had said.

Morgan fanned herself and checked the room's thermostat. "I know," she said, agreeing with Alexis's assessment of the city's heat. Moving from the thermostat to the mirror over the dresser, she pulled a pink halter over her head and threw it to the floor. "It must be at least eighty-five degrees out there, and it's ten o'clock at night. Can you imagine what it's going to feel like tomorrow afternoon?"

"I don't know and I don't care, because I plan to be lying in the bed getting a nice long nap to rest up for the concert tomorrow," Claire said, applying black eyeliner to her right eye. The twelve-dollar pencil made her already large, almond-shaped eyes look even bigger. The white low-cut dress she wore looked fabulous against her Hershey-brown skin, and with her short pixie cut, Claire knew that she would be the talk of the town that night.

After much thought, Alexis had decided on a much more understated look. Her outfit consisted of an orange halter tunic, snug-fitting jeans and strapped tan stiletto sandals; it was simple but sexy. Alexis arranged her hair in loose curls that brushed her neck, applied eyeliner, mascara, moisturizer and lip gloss and was ready to go in under forty-five minutes. Morgan, on the other hand, was still engaged in a marathon of clothes selection, and the once-immaculate hotel room looked as if a hurricane had blown through it. A slew of clothes, shoes and hair products were strewn about, and three very different perfume scents filled the air.

As soon as their plane had touched down in New Orleans, the ladies had been ready to experience everything the city had to offer, wanting nothing less than letting loose and partying. Claire turned on the radio in their rented SUV to find out what was happening on the club scene that weekend. In just a few minutes of listening, they had learned that the House of Blues was the hot spot for the evening.

As Alexis began transferring essential items from her everyday purse to a tan clutch, Morgan was pulling a yellow spaghetti-strap mini-dress over her head and smiling in the mirror. After fluffing her shoulder-length curly hair, applying lipstick and strapping her gold high-heeled sandals around her ankles, she grabbed the matching purse and declared herself ready to go.

On the short drive to the House of Blues through the historic streets of New Orleans, the three friends recognized some of the city's landmarks, planning to see more of them during their trip. The speakers in the SUV blared Destiny's Child, and when the song "Through With Love" began to play, Alexis lifted her hand up in the air, swaying with the beat and proclaiming the song her new anthem.

"I wonder how long this little act you have going on is going to last?" Claire asked Alexis, who was loudly repeating the words to the song as if she were the fourth member of the group.

"This is no act. This is the new me, and I hereby declare that I am through with love." Alexis sang along as Morgan pulled the SUV in front of the club. She kept singing even as the valet opened the door and helped her step down onto the pavement.

"Look, why don't we leave the singing to the professionals and just enjoy ourselves. This is supposed to be *the* spot tonight, so let's get a table, order some drinks and meet some men," Claire said, positioning herself between Alexis and Morgan as they hurried up the club's walkway. The moment they left the humid New Orleans air behind and stepped into the cool air-conditioned entranceway of the House of Blues, Alexis fell under the seductive spell of the nightclub and forgot the song she had been singing and promised herself to have a good time.

The club had been open less than an hour, but the dance floor was already packed. Couples were bumping, grinding and swaying to the music of Usher. There were people everywhere and as the three made their way across the club, Alexis got lost in the crowd until Morgan grabbed her arm and led her to a table overlooking the dance floor.

"Girl, look at all these men," Claire said excitedly, looking around the dimly lit club at the throngs of men who were standing at the bar, dancing or scattered about the club talking to various women. Alexis had to admit there were a lot of handsome and sexy men in the club that night. But she promised herself that she would not stray from her resolution; she was through with love and planned to keep her vow come hell or high water.

"Welcome to the House of Blues, ladies. Can I get you anything to drink tonight?" a waitress in a black HOB uniform asked, placing three black cocktail napkins on the square table.

Morgan ordered an apple martini. Claire asked for a chocolate martini for herself and then ordered a screaming orgasm for Alexis. "She *really* needs one," Claire told the waitress, leaning close to her. Both women looked at Alexis as if she were some kind of charity case.

"You know what, Claire? You are truly an asshole. Why would you say something like that?" Alexis griped after the waitress retreated. She was agitated, and had Claire not been one of her oldest and dearest friends, she would have punched her in the mouth.

"It was just a joke; don't be so sensitive."

"Excuse me, ladies, but the gentlemen in the corner would like to purchase your drinks for you," the waitress said, returning to their table before going to the bar. Alexis, Morgan and Claire looked over at the dark corner where two men sat. Seeing the women looking at them, they smiled broadly, revealing entire top rows of gold teeth.

"Oh, hell no!" Claire blurted loudly.

"Could you please tell the gentlemen that we do appreciate the gesture, but that we would really prefer pay for our own drinks," Alexis said, attempting to cover for Claire's tactless outburst. The waitress took the message back to the men.

"They are not the kind of guys I planned on meeting down here," Claire said, wiping tears of laughter from her eyes.

A crowd of mostly female club goers rushing the entrance prompted the three women to crane to see what the commotion was all about. "Where in the world are all those women rushing to?" Alexis asked, half in an attempt to get a better view.

The crowd parted like the Red Sea as five men nearly as tall as the archway they had just passed through stepped forward. The women, most of them clad in nothing more than what looked like underwear, were standing around them like little lost puppies and shamelessly making complete asses of themselves.

"Look at those hoes," Claire said, standing up so she could see over the crowd.

"Are you trying to get a better look at the hoes or at who the hoes are falling all over?" Morgan asked, thanking the waitress and taking a sip of her green-apple martini.

"Both."

The waitress placed Alexis's screaming orgasm on her napkin and turned to Claire. "They play for the Hornets. I've seen them in here a couple of times, but not too often, mostly for special events and stuff."

As the waitress left to take other orders, Claire licked her lips and checked her cleavage.

"I know you are not about to try to talk to them?" Alexis hissed in disbelief. She reached across the table and grabbed Claire by the wrist, pulling her back into her seat.

"I most certainly am going to talk to them. Why shouldn't I?" Claire stood again, smoothed out the tiny wrinkles in her dress and sauntered toward the five men.

"I don't know what makes her think that she can just walk over there and get these guys to talk with her. I mean, look at all those women. There's no way that she's going to get their attention." Morgan took another sip of her martini and watched doubtfully as a determined Claire neared the men.

"You know Claire. She normally gets exactly what she wants, so I wouldn't be surprised if she came over here with those guys following *her* like puppy dogs."

Alexis and Morgan watched Claire pushing the crowd of hyperactive women and stood right in front of one of the players. She shook his hand, said a few words and then pointed over to their table. Four of the five players standing with Claire at the entrance looked to see the women at the table she had pointed out. The fifth was so enthralled by Claire that he couldn't take his eyes off her.

Alexis and Morgan looked disbelievingly at each other as their friend led all five men past the under-dressed, open-mouthed groupies and over to their table. "I really hope Claire didn't let them think we were going to do something to them to get them to come over here," Alexis declared, unconsciously smoothing her hair.

"I don't even want to talk to them. My man is waiting for me at home. I don't need any distractions," Morgan said, reaching into her purse. She pulled out a small com-pact and checked her makeup.

"Okay, gentlemen, I would like to introduce you to my friends. This," Claire said, tapping Morgan's shoulder, "is Morgan." Morgan put on a smile so big and bright Alexis could practically see her see reflection in it. It seems it hadn't her taken long to forget about her man waiting at home. "And this is Alexis," Claire continued with a flourish.

Alexis looked up, way up, and her eyes landed on the most beautiful man she had ever seen. Of course, she had thought the same thing about Kevin the first time she had seen him, too, but this man was different. She thought he was truly a work of art. When their eyes met and he smiled, showing the deepest, most perfect dimples she had ever seen, she thought that she would fall out of her seat. Just looking at him made her panties wet, and it took all the self-control she could muster not to jump into his arms, run her fingers through his curly, tapered afro and proclaim her love.

"Is it all right if I sit here?" the Adonis asked, pulling out the seat next to her and flashing that million-dollar smile at her again.

"Go ahead," she answered in just above a whisper, trying to regain the composure she had lost the minute this man entered her space. Though she was totally mesmerized, in the background she could faintly hear Claire humming her short lived "anthem" *Through With Love.*

The other men pulled chairs up to the table and introduced themselves. Alexis failed to hear any of their names, so enthralled was she by the mere presence of this man. The scent of his cologne and the warmth emitting from his body were almost too much for her to handle. So she excused herself from the group and fled for the restroom.

"Alexis?" Claire was at the stall door less than twenty seconds after she had locked herself inside. "Alexis, what in the world is your problem? You act like you can't put a sentence together."

Alexis came out of the stall and faced her friend. "Girl, that man."

"Girl, all those men, but, yeah, I hear you. The one that keeps smiling at you is extra fine with his golden skin and curly hair. Did you hear me humming your anthem? I was trying to say I told you so."

"There is no need for any 'I told you so' because I'm sticking to what I said in the car. I'm absolutely done with men, and I don't care how good this guy looks or how delicious he smells, I am not falling for it. I'm done." Alexis slammed her hand on the sink counter for emphasis.

"Are you trying to convince me or yourself? Because to me it sounds like the latter."

"I'm not trying to convince anybody; I'm simply stating fact."

"Okay, fine then. If that is the truth, why are you hiding out in here?"

"I'm not hiding. I was refreshing my makeup."

"For Massai?"

"Who's Massai?" Alexis asked, baffled.

"The guy sitting next to you. You know, the one who you would never get with under any circumstances."

Alexis couldn't believe she had been so awestruck she hadn't heard his name. "Well, it really doesn't matter to me what his name is, and no I was absolutely not refreshing my makeup for him."

"Okay, Alexis, whatever you say," Claire responded opening the door to the restroom and returning into the main club area. Alexis followed and as she approached the table, Massai favored her with another gorgeous smile. She took a deep breath, telling herself, *Do not fall for this man, no matter how fine is.*

Claire sat down next to her newfound friend and Alexis returned to her seat next to Massai. Morgan was no longer at the table. Her two friends saw the totally "committed" Morgan dropping it like it was hot on the dance floor. Claire and Malik, along with the other guy who's name Alexis still didn't know, took to the dance floor when a Lil' Jon song began blasting through the speakers, leaving Alexis and Massai alone at the table. Being alone with him made her nervous; she almost didn't trust herself around him. She decided that the only way she would be able to control her hormones around him was to behave as if he wasn't sitting there.

"Claire says that you guys are out here for your birthday," he said, scooting his chair closer to Alexis so he could be heard over the club's thumping bass.

"Yeah."

"How old are you?"

"Twenty-five."

"And you are going to the Music Fest tomorrow?"

"Yeah."

Massai shifted uncomfortably and signaled the waitress, who was a couple of tables away. "Aren't you a woman of a thousand words?" he said sarcastically.

Alexis averted her eyes and she, too, shifted in her seat.

"What can I get for you?" the waitress asked, taking a pen and pad from her apron pocket.

"I'll just have a Corona with lime and—" he turned to Alexis. "Would you like anything?" she shook her head no. Meanwhile, her friends were living it up on the dance floor while she was sitting at this table with a dream of a man, a stubborn ego and a hardened heart.

"Are you always this quiet or is tonight special?" Massai asked after the waitress had disappeared into the crowd.

"I don't mean to be rude."

"That's a surprise."

Alexis and Massai sat and listened to at least two more songs before exchanging another word.

"So what do you do?" Massai asked as a Luther Vandross song began to play. Alexis watched as his friends pulled Morgan and Claire close and swayed to the beat. She realized that this man was refusing to give up, and she would have to work that much harder to discourage him.

"What do I do?"

"For a living?" Massai clarified, taking a gulp of his Corona.

"I teach fifth grade."

Whereupon Massai responded, "If I had a teacher like you when I was in fifth grade, I would have gotten better grades."

"I can't even count the number of times I've heard that," Alexis said, laughing out loud.

"Okay, so it *was* a little lame; I was just trying to get you to smile. But the compliment still stands; you really are beautiful."

Although Alexis tried to fight it, she felt her cheeks heating up and knew that she was blushing. Massai noticed and gave her one of those dimpled smiles.

"What are you doing tomorrow afternoon before the concert? Why don't we get together and I can show you around New Orleans?" He took her response to his compliment to mean he could move forward.

"I don't think that would be such a good idea."

"And why not?"

"Because I just got out of a bad relationship, and I came to New Orleans to hear some good music and shop," she said, gulping down her drink and feeling a little dizzy as a result.

"It's just a tour, not hot, butt-naked sex. Anyway, I have a girlfriend." Taking another sip of his beer, he returned to watching the couples on the dance floor.

"If you have a girlfriend, why are you asking me out?"

"Because I was trying to be nice. You do know what that word means, don't you? I'm sure you do, even though you are showing me no evidence of such knowledge now. You know what? I think I'll leave you and your attitude alone. Have a *nice* evening." And with that, Massai grabbed his beer, and strolled over to the opposite side of the club. Alexis watched him retreat, feeling confused and alone and hoping she hadn't sworn off men too soon and wouldn't live to regret her words. Maybe she had been a tad too hasty.

6

OPTIONS

Massai and Malik took deep breaths and exhaled to clear their lungs of smoke as they came out of the House of Blues and onto the curb at three in the morning. The party was still in full swing, but once Claire and her friends left, Malik lost interest in the club. Besides Massai was his ride home, so he had no choice but to follow. Angelo, Marcus, and Stacey, the teammates they originally had come with, decided to stay, taking a handful of women up to the infamous Foundation Room.

"What's going on with you and the girl in the orange?" Malik asked, pulling his cellphone from his back pocket and checking the missed-call log. Massai shrugged and handed the claim ticket to the valet. "Well, I'm just asking because since you and Eva have been together I have never once seen you trying to talk to another woman. I thought Eva had you under lock and key."

"I wouldn't say all that."

"I would. You let that hoe spend all your money, stay out all night and you have no idea where she is or what she's doing. All this and you don't say one word. Not one! I mean you have the best-looking women dropping their panties for you on the road and you won't even open the door." Malik replaced his cellphone and shook his head with disbelief and pity.

"I am not into sleeping around with a whole bunch of women when I'm in a committed relationship."

"Now you're just sounding like a woman. 'I'm in a committed relationship'," Malik mocked. "Half the team are in committed relationships, and you don't see them turning anybody away."

The valet parked Massai's silver Mercedes G500 SUV at the curb, hopped out and held the door open. He handed him a twenty-dollar bill, slid into the driver's seat and waited for Malik to slide in next to him. Then they took off down Decatur Street.

"And you think that's okay?" Massai asked, reaching over to turn on the radio.

"No. Actually, I don't think it's okay, but I do think it's normal. Not only are we men, but we're professional athletes. We are expected to get ours whether we have a wife, girlfriend, baby's momma or all three."

"That's just not me. I know Eva and I have our issues, but I couldn't cheat on her. My mama didn't raise me to treat women that way."

"Did she raise you to close your eyes to the obvious and get played in the process? I would be willing to put some money on the fact that Eva is probably giving it up to any Tom, Dick and Harry with an AmEx card. I hope you're strapping up."

"When would Eva have the time to cheat on me? All she does is shop."

"And that's a problem all of its own. I'm almost positive that she is out there doing a hell of a lot more than shopping. That's all you think she does. And why are you being so naïve about this girl? You act like you grew up in a cave or something. You know most women get dollar signs in their eyes whenever they look at someone like us. Eva is no exception."

Massai couldn't comment. Though he hated to admit it, he knew Malik had a point. The longer he and Eva were a couple, the more time she spent shopping and the less time she devoted to nurturing their relationship.

"You're thinking about it, aren't you?" Malik asked, a triumphant smile on his chocolate-colored face. "My point is this: keep your options open. The little babe in the orange is definitely an option."

"Alexis is hardly an option."

"That's her name? Sexy, lexy."

"She's one of those bitter-ass women. Fine as hell, but bitter. And she lives in Detroit."

"No one is saying that you have to marry her. Just take her around town and try to get to know her. Leave Eva's ass at home wondering where *you* are for a change."

Massai came to the end of the long dirt road that led to Malik's eight-bedroom home and made a left turn.

"I asked her out while we were alone at the table and she said no."

"Oh, so she *is* an option?"

"I'm not going to sit up here and lie to you. Yes, I'm interested, but she isn't, so that's that."

"You're a quitter."

"I'm not a quitter, and I'm definitely not a beggar. I have too much other stuff going on in my life right now to have to beg some woman to let me show her around."

"Okay, it's your choice, but if I were in your position there is no way in the world I would pass up someone who looked like that." With that, Malik jumped out of the car and jogged up the walkway to his front door.

Malik had given Massai a lot to think about. They had been friends since they met at a basketball camp in junior high school, Massai in the sixth grade and Malik, being a year older, in the seventh. That was nearly fourteen years ago, and ever since, the two had been the best of friends as well as the fiercest of competitors. Both were signed by different universities in different states; deciding to stay close to home, Massai attended Duke University, while Malik signed with Syracuse in New York a year earlier. The hundreds of miles between them did not end their friendship and they spoke often, sometimes two to three times a week. Their favorite and most intense games were when their schools competed on the basketball court. It was only by chance that the two ended up playing for the same NBA team. Malik left school after his sophomore year to enter the NBA draft. He was picked up by the Memphis Grizzlies and played for them the first three years of his career. Massai, on the other hand, finished a degree in communications before leaving Duke and entering the draft. He was a first-round pick that year for the New Orleans Hornets, and it was during that time that Malik was traded to the same team. That was two years and approximately two hundred serious conversations ago.

In many of those conversations, especially recently, Malik expressed concerns regarding Massai's girlfriend. He remembered the first time he introduced Eva to his best friend. Malik was very polite and courteous in front of her, but the next day at practice he pulled him aside to tell him exactly what he thought of his new love interest.

"We've been friends for a long time, and I'm saying this only out of concern. I think that she is manipulative and an opportunist. I think she's with you only for the zeros in your bank account, and you are going to end up getting screwed."

Massai didn't want to believe it then, but he was definitely beginning to believe it now. During the past six months, things seemed to be changing drastically between the two. When they first began dating a year and a half ago, Eva completely catered to him. After games, she would run his bath and give him long hot-oil massages. Back then she often refused the expensive gifts he tried to shower on her, and opted for shopping trips at quirky second-hand shops rather than at New Orleans' expensive boutiques. It wasn't until Massai began his second year in the NBA that Eva quit her nursing job and began staying out all night, spending his money like water. It had become routine for him to receive a massive credit card bill for just one afternoon of what Eva referred to as light shopping. Just last week, she returned home showing off a full-length chinchilla fur coat she purchased with the help of Massai's credit card. When he questioned her about the cost of the coat Eva asked sweetly, "It was half price at a summer sale and besides, don't you want me to have nice things?"

There was something about her—the way she spoke with such honey in her voice and the warmth of her body when she pressed it up against him—that made Massai feel powerless. It was as if she had him under some kind of hypnosis that prevented him from thinking logically and clearly.

He steered his SUV into the circular driveway and pressed the garage-door opener stored in the center console. The door rose slowly, revealing the rest of his automobiles: a candy-apple red Ferrari Enzo and a black metallic BMW 745. A custom-made Ducati motorcycle rounded out his collection of expensive vehicles. The cars were parked there day after day, but they still gave him pleasure each time he saw them. It was hard to believe that a little dusty boy from Charlotte, North Carolina, could grow up to have all this.

Massai parked the BMW and hopped out. Then he noticed Eva's car missing from its spot. He had surprised her with a custom-made Chrysler Crossfire for Valentine's Day, but after a fit of tears and door slamming, Massai caved and followed her down to the Lexus dealership and purchased an indigo ink pearl SC430. He sent the Crossfire to his seventeen-year-old sister, Melissa, in Charlotte, calling it an early graduation gift. In hindsight, he should have left her then. But hindsight is twenty-twenty.

His watch read three forty-five. He couldn't believe that Eva was still out this late. It was not the first time, but it was upsetting, nevertheless. Closing the door behind him, he entered the laundry room. Piles of dirty laundry that Eva promised to wash were still in hampers on the floor, untouched. He went through the kitchen and family room and then took the main staircase up to the master bedroom suite. The normally immaculate bedroom bore a striking resemblance to the laundry room; Eva's clothes were scattered all the over the bed and on the carpeted floor. He collected the clothes and left them in a pile at the doorway, hoping that when she finally got home she would see the clothes, get his pointed message and do what she had promised.

Stepping out of his khaki shorts and polo-style shirt, Massai made his way to the master bathroom and opened the glass shower door. He turned the spout to its hottest setting. Once the entire room was filled with steam, he pulled off his boxer shorts and white undershirt and stood under the scalding-hot water. Most people would receive third-degree burns from water at this temperature, but he loved the feel of the hot water streaming over his stiff muscles. Especially after a very physical game, he would come home and spend up to an hour and a half in the shower.

Suddenly he felt a blast of cold air. Eva, half dressed in a purple ensemble that showed more skin than it covered, was holding the shower door open and smiling at him.

"Can you close the door, please? You're letting all the steam out," he complained, reaching for the shower knob and turning it to the right, causing another showerhead to rain water on to the top of his head.

"Is that any way to greet me? You haven't seen me since nine this morning, and all you can say is shut the shower door?" she retorted, slamming the shower door but not leaving the bathroom. "And did you even notice my new dress?"

"Did you even notice what time you were walking into my house?"

"Oh, so now it's your house?"

"Well, as far as I know I am the only one who pays any bills around here."

"I think I pull my own weight," Eva said, again opening the shower door. She had removed her dress and stood in front of Massai wearing nothing but a pout.

Looking at her nearly perfect body, he felt a tingle but refused to give into the sensation. "You cannot fix everything by taking off your clothes."

"And why not?" Eva reached for the soap and began lathering his body from head to toe.

"Don't you realize we're in an adult relationship? I am not some horny teenager who can't think straight when he sees a naked woman. We have serious problems that need to be talked about if we want this relationship to work."

"Oh, Massai, I think that's part of the problem. You are too serious. Why can't you just enjoy what's happening right now?"

He cocked his head skeptically and watched the soap lather leave his body and wash down the drain. Deep down, he knew that was where his relationship was heading as well.

"I just want you to be happy. I love you. I just think you're stressed, and I know just the thing to make you feel better . . ."

Massai stood still as Eva slowly dropped to her knees and opened her mouth wide. Taking him into her mouth, she began to suck just the way he liked it, and he felt powerless to stop her. It wasn't until he filled her mouth and watched her swallow that he realized he never had the chance to ask her where she had been or whom she'd been with all night.

7

CELLPHONE CONVERSATIONS

"I really don't understand you, Alexis," Claire said over beignets and coffee with chicory at the famous New Orleans eatery, Café du Monde.

"What are you talking about?" she asked, although she already had a pretty good idea. Her treatment of Massai had been a hot topic of conversation since they left the House of Blues.

She herself had to admit that she was attracted to him, but Alexis knew firsthand that attraction wasn't enough. Attraction had gotten her burned more times than she could count, and she was not interested in being hurt. Not now, or ever again.

"I don't understand why you treated Massai the way you did, especially when you were so obviously into him."

"As I have told you repeatedly, I am not getting involved with anybody. Not to mention the very important fact that he has a girlfriend."

"So the issue here isn't the fact that your choices in men have been disastrous, but that this one has a girlfriend?" Morgan chimed in.

"None of it is an issue because I am not interested in him."

"Yeah, right."

"I'm serious. You thought I was mean to him? You should have heard the way he spoke to me. He said that I have a nasty attitude."

"You do," Claire agreed, adding a drop of cream to her coffee.

"This is how I look at your situation—" Morgan began.

"I really don't care how you look at my situation because it is *my* situation and I don't recall asking for your input, Morgan," Alexis said, becoming fed up with the entire subject.

"See what I mean? Nasty attitude," Claire laughed, pulling her ringing cellphone from her purse and pressing the talk button.

Alexis threw up her hands in surrender and reluctantly let Morgan finish her point.

"I was just trying to say that you always fall so fast for all the wrong guys, and maybe because of that you're doing everything in your power not to like this one. Who knows? He could be Mr. Right."

"Or at least Mr. Right Now," Claire chimed in after saying a few words to her caller and snapping her cellphone shut. "Think of it like this, Alexis: We're in New Orleans and along comes this guy who is tall, handsome and painfully sexy. Who better to rid you of your broken heart, even if it is just on a short-term basis?"

"I can't think of anyone better," Morgan said, adding her two cents.

"Look, as I told you before, there is no way anything will be happening between Massai and me. And frankly,

I really don't understand why you two keep bringing it up." Alexis leaned back in her chair and folded her arms across her chest defensively. She glared at her friends and without opening her mouth, dared them to risk further comment on her love life.

Alexis reached for her coffee mug, lifting it up and then putting it back down without taking a sip. "And even if I were interested in him, which I'm not, it really doesn't matter because I'll never see him again, anyway. We met at a club and that was that."

"I have Malik's number. Why don't I call him, and we could all go out after the concert tonight. See the city, get something to eat?" Claire offered the invitation as innocently as possible.

"He has a girlfriend, Claire."

"And if he didn't?"

"If he didn't have a girlfriend, I still wouldn't let you call him."

"Well, what if I told you that was Malik on the phone just a minute ago?"

"You're lying," Alexis countered. Her voice cracked and she looked from Claire to Morgan, attempting to accurately read their thoughts.

"No, I'm not. I gave him my number last night and told him to call me if he and his boys wanted to get together with us sometime while we were here."

"Morgan, is she telling the truth?" Alexis asked, the heat beginning to rise from her body in anger and nervousness.

Morgan didn't speak, nodding yes instead.

"Why would you do that?" Alexis whined.

"I like him. I think he's cute and fun and rich and I want to have a good time while I'm here. Everything isn't always about you."

Alexis sat back in her chair again and sighed. While she knew that Claire was telling the truth and genuinely felt happy that her friend had found someone she could vibe with so quickly, she was nevertheless concerned about what Claire's newfound friendship meant for her and her declaration of emotional and sexual independence.

Alexis knew that something was going on. Morgan and Claire were tiptoeing around the room and speaking in hushed tones, and she was sure they were trying to hide something from her.

After stuffing themselves at brunch, the women left the café and decided to skip the sightseeing they had planned for the afternoon and go back to the hotel and relax before the concert. On the walk back, and even afterwards, Claire kept dropping not-so-subtle hints about Alexis and Massai, even once mentioning that they may be running into each other in the very near future.

Once in their hotel room the ladies spent the next three hours sleeping, until they heard Morgan's raised voice through the closed bathroom door.

"Nothing is going on, Craig!" her friends heard her yell in desperation.

"He knows just what to say to upset her." Claire sat up in bed and rubbed her eyes. She was referring to the way Craig would often attempt to sabotage Morgan's plans by throwing guilt trips her way. Even though she knew that she wasn't doing anything wrong, Craig would nevertheless make her feel as if spending time with her friends and doing things that she enjoyed was wrong.

"I don't know why she stays with him. There has got to be a point when she says enough is enough!" Alexis reasoned, searching through the suitcase she had hastily packed back in Detroit.

"I wish she would wake up and realize that Craig only does that when he's doing wrong himself. He's one of those men who put what he is doing on someone else to make himself seem innocent."

"He's manipulative. I think she is the one you need to set up while we're out here. A good man, or at least a good time, could do her some good right about now," Alexis commented, rejecting a black wrap-around dress and resuming her search.

"I think you're right, but I'm not giving up on you, either. You deserve some happiness, Alexis."

She knew that her friend was right. She wanted nothing more in this world than to live a happy, fulfilling, purpose-driven life, but accomplishing these goals required her to put her heart on the line and be open to possibilities. That was something she was not willing to do.

"That's it!" Morgan declared as she slammed the bathroom door shut behind her and tossed her cellphone across the room.

"What is it?" Alexis asked, looking over her shoulder at Morgan.

"I am sick of trying to be the perfect girlfriend. I have to put forth all this effort, and all he does is try to keep me down."

"I thought you two had the perfect relationship and were going to be together forever," Claire reminded her, snuggling back under the covers.

"Sometimes we do have the perfect relationship, but other times he makes me want to push him off a cliff." Morgan sat on the couch and held her head in her hands. "I have decided to have a good time and not worry about what he's going to say or think. Maybe I'll meet somebody like the two of you did— someone I can really get into."

"Excuse me? I did not meet anybody I can really get into. I think that's Claire you're referring to," Alexis quickly corrected her.

"Would you come off it? This 'I am going to be dickless and celibate for the rest of my life' act is getting really old, really quick. Why can't you just admit that you are interested in Massai? We're your friends, and there is absolutely no point in lying to us."

"I'm not lying. How could I be interested in someone I don't even know?"

"It only takes seconds to look at someone and size him up. It only took *you* a second to practically do a Flo Jo into the bathroom last night when you looked at Massai," Claire added. She had stayed out of the conversation but, like Morgan, was getting a little sick of Alexis denying the obvious.

"I had something in my eye."

"More like in your panties."

Alexis was silent. She had been beaten again and knew that nothing she could say would convince her friends that Massai was the furthest thing from her mind. After all, how could she make someone believe something that she didn't fully believe herself?

With only an hour and a half to dress and to get the concert, and with only one bathroom, the three friends raced around the room pulling outfits together and vying for mirror space. Alexis, as always, was the first one dressed and was forced to wait while Claire and Morgan argued over the mirror.

At ten minutes to seven, Claire's cellphone rang and a huge smile appeared on her face. Alexis saw this and was confused and curious; she had never seen a phone call make Claire smile that way.

"Hi," Claire said, holding the phone between her ear and shoulder as she finished painting her nails with red polish. "Yes, we're ready."

Alexis glared at Claire and sensed something suspicious in the air. She hadn't made plans for anyone to join them at the concert, so she couldn't understand to whom Claire was talking, as if there was a prearranged meeting of some kind.

"Okay, we'll be right down." Claire pressed the end button on her phone and tossed it into her purse. She smiled knowingly at Morgan. "Are we ready?"

"Who were you talking to?" Alexis asked, taking one last look in the mirror.

The three were in the hallway and walking towards the elevator before Alexis realized that she hadn't received an answer. "Did you hear me? Who were you talking to?" Alexis asked again pushing the elevator's down button.

"I thought I left my mama back in Detroit."

They got on the elevator with Alexis still pressing for an answer. "I'm not trying to sound like your mother; I was just wondering who you were talking to. If it's not a big deal, why are you getting so defensive?"

The elevator stopped three floors from the lobby and three middle-aged women stepped inside, chattering excitedly. Looking at them, Alexis smiled and imagined herself, twenty years from now, still traveling with Claire and Morgan.

"It's not a big deal, but I just don't understand why you are trying to be all in my business."

"Well, if you're talking about us going with you, then I would think it was our business. Wouldn't you, Morgan?" Alexis turned to Morgan for support. Instead of agreeing with her friend, Morgan simply shrugged and kept her eyes on the illuminated numbers on the elevator's main panel.

"Will you just relax?" Claire pleaded, looking directly at Alexis as the elevator doors opened and the older women strutted into the lobby.

"Okay, fine! I was just asking you a question."

The three got off the elevator and walked toward the huge double doors facing Bourbon Street.

"This concert is going to be—" Alexis began, trying to lighten the mood. She stopped in mid-sentence. In front of her stood Massai.

8

ROUGH RIDE

Alexis seemed glued in place, her gold ballet slippers refusing to leave the ground. She watched in stony silence as Malik kissed Claire on the cheek and then introduced his cousin Orlando to Morgan. Massai and Alexis eye-balled one another but said nothing.

"Are you coming?" Claire called out as everyone got into Malik's eggshell colored Bentley. Alexis humphed, then brushed past Massai and walked quickly toward the car to join the others. "No, you'll have to ride with Massai. There isn't any room for you. It only seats four."

She looked from the occupants of the car to Massai and then back again. "There is no way I'm riding with him," she said coldly, pointing at him with disgust. Her voice said she was steadfast and focused, but on the inside she was becoming as shaky as a bowl of Jell-O.

"Fine with me," he said, walking to his car and opening the driver's side door. "Let her walk."

Alexis stubbornly stood on the sidewalk between the two cars, her arms crossed. She was painfully aware she was being childish, but she also knew that if forced to ride with him, there was no telling what would happen.

"You're being ridiculous, Alexis. Would you please get in the car?"

"I'll drive the rental and meet you there."

"There is no gas in the rental, and nobody is going to wait for you to get any. Just get in the car with Massai and let's get going before we miss Floetry," Morgan pleaded, sticking her head out of the back passenger-side window.

Although angry, she gave in, realizing she really didn't have a choice. By the time she would have gotten the car out of the hotel's garage, stopped for gas and found her way to the New Orleans Superdome, she probably would have missed the entire first half of the show. Defeated, she walked to the BMW and yanked the locked door handle, nearly ripping off three French manicured nails in the process.

"Can you please unlock the door?"

"Oh, would you like a ride?" Massai rolled down the passenger's side window and asked sarcastically. He gave her the dimpled smile that had made her weak last night, but unlike twenty-four hours ago, this one was tinged with sarcasm.

"Yes. I would drive myself, but I don't want to be late."

"Don't you think you should apologize to me?"

Alexis moved away from the car and folded her arms. She was too stubborn to give in so easily. He revved the engine and put the car into gear. Just as he looked in his rear-view mirror and prepared to pull out into traffic she blurted out, "Sorry!"

"That didn't sound very sincere. Try it again," he instructed, revving the engine again.

"Will you just open the damn door?" she yelled, causing passersby to stop and stare.

Massai laughed at her agitation and unlocked the automatic doors.

Alexis slid in beside him and glared. "I just want to make something clear from jump. This is not a date. We are just two people riding together to a concert."

He didn't comment, instead pulling out from his parking spot so fast the car's tires squealed and Alexis's head hit the car's leather headrest. She rubbed the back of her head but didn't comment.

The two rode in silence for a few minutes, with Alexis secretly admiring the way his muscles rippled when he shifted gears and Massai telling himself not to reach over and touch her soft shoulder. Her white spaghetti strap had slipped off her shoulder and her gold chandelier earrings were caressing her caramel skin. He was stealing looks at her when he should have been concentrating on the road. As he licked his lips thinking about kissing her, Alexis's voice snapped him back from fantasy to reality.

"How's your girlfriend? What's her name again?"

"Eva. Her name is Eva, and she's fine."

"She must be very understanding. I mean, with you going out every night."

"I do not go out every night."

"Seems that way to me. In my opinion, you go out way too much to have a girlfriend waiting at home."

"You met me last night, so please don't think your opinion holds any weight with me. And Eva is not the type to wait at home for anyone."

"Oh, so she's a party girl?"

"You could say that." Waiting for a red light to change, Massai looked over at Alexis and asked, "Why are you so concerned about my relationship, anyway? You didn't even want to ride with me in the first place, and you have made it perfectly clear that this isn't a date, so why don't you just sit back and keep your mouth shut?"

"You don't have to be rude. I was only trying to make small talk."

He laughed. "You can dish it out, but you can't take it, right?"

"Just forget it, okay? You drive, I'll keep quiet and we'll get along just fine."

"What's wrong with you? You're too pretty to act so ugly," Massai said. He was in fact awestruck by her beauty. In all his years and out of all the women he had come into contact with, he had never seen someone as beautiful as Alexis. Since he met her the night before, he thought of little else and, even though he didn't want to admit it, her sarcastic humor and snippy attitude kept him on his toes and deepened his attraction.

"Nothing is wrong with me. What's wrong with you?"

"So you mean to tell me that you act like this all the time?"

"Act like what?"

"Like nobody taught you how to be sociable, polite; like you have no home training."

"I have plenty of home training. I just don't see a reason to be polite to you when you aren't being polite to me."

"Alexis, are you serious? I tried to be polite to you last night and where did that get me? I tried to be polite today, and you acted like I'm some kind of criminal. You didn't even want to ride with me."

"I know as a professional athlete you are used to women throwing themselves at you, but I'm not that type. I am not a groupie, and I'm not going to fall all over you because you can put a ball through a hoop."

"There you go. My playing ball for a living has absolutely nothing to do with *you* having a nasty attitude."

"I do not have a nasty attitude."

"My mother raised me to treat others like I want to be treated. I don't know how your parents raised you." His insinuation was clear.

"So now my parents ain't shit?"

"If the shoe fits."

"You're an ass," Alexis hissed, feeling her blood boil in her veins.

"And you're a—"

"A what?" she asked, cutting Massai off before he could finish the insult. "If you were getting ready to call me out of my name, then you can pull this car over right now. Don't think I won't fight a man; I don't care how tall you are," she fumed. "You know, Massai, here I am thinking that you're so cute and such a gentleman, but you are just like all the other guys."

"So you think I'm cute?" he asked, sitting up a little straighter in the driver's seat and flashing his signature smile.

"No, I *thought* you were cute. Past tense. Now I just think that you're a jerk."

They sat quietly for the rest of the ride; the only sound in the car came from the stereo system. Finally, the Superdome loomed before them, and Alexis silently thanked God that this experience was half over.

Massai steered the car into a parking spot next to Malik's Bentley. He turned off the radio and cut the engine, and then he removed the keys from the ignition and sat with his hands in his lap. She was halfway out the door, one foot in the parking-lot pavement and the other poised to follow. "Aren't you coming?" Alexis asked, glancing back at him.

When he didn't answer, she shrugged and was about to make her escape when his strong hand closed around her wrist. "Alexis, wait."

Her gut reaction was to yank her hand away, but she looked into his eyes and felt a tingle shoot through her arm as she stopped and paid attention. "Close the door," Massai directed, never taking his eyes off her. She felt hypnotized and powerless and instantly closed the door. She looked to her right and saw Claire and Morgan staring at her strangely. Claire was mouthing, "Are you okay?" With a nod of her head, she assured her friends that she was indeed okay. The foursome started walking toward the Superdome to give them some privacy. Alexis then turned back to Massai, anxious to hear what he had to say.

"Alexis, I want to be completely honest with you right now. I'm not sure how you are going to react to this, but I'm going to let you know, anyway, because I think that it needs to be said." He took a deep breath and continued. "I'm really feeling you, Alexis. I know I have a girlfriend and all that, and I don't want to sound corny or rehearsed, but I can't help the way I feel. I have been thinking about you nonstop since the second I got up from your table last night. When you said that women probably don't talk to me the way you did, you were absolutely right, but the women who don't challenge me are only interested in my bank account."

Alexis took a deep breath. She didn't trust herself to respond, so she decided to wait for him to continue.

"All I'm asking you is for a chance, Alexis. I want to get to know you, and I want you to get to know me, but you're not making it easy. Can you just let down this brick wall that you have around yourself?" He loosened his grip on her wrist and softly intertwined his fingers with hers.

She looked down and felt a jolt that shot from the hand he was holding all the way up to her heart. No one had held her hand like that since high school, and she thought it the sweetest, most innocent and pure gesture—both then and now. And though the gesture made her slightly weak in the knees, Alexis was stubborn and her heart had been hardened. She could not let go of the pain and disappointment she had experienced with an assortment of men. She withdrew her hand from his, breaking the spell he had cast over her.

"Massai, you have a girlfriend. I do not knowingly get involved with men who are in relationships."

"All I'm asking is for you to give me a chance."

Alexis looked at Massai, over her shoulder to Claire and Morgan, who waited patiently in the parking lot for her, and then back again. Giving Massai a chance would entail letting down her guard, and she had a feeling that once she let down her guard around this man it would be only a matter of time before she gave him exactly what he wanted. So without answering, she hopped out of the car and joined her friends, leaving him confused but not ready to give up.

9

THE AFTER-PARTY

"What the hell is going on with you?" Claire demanded. They were in the first floor bathroom of Malik's ten-bathroom home. The concert had ended over an hour ago but no one was ready for the night to end, so when Malik suggested that they pick up some po' boy sandwiches and come back to his place, Claire and Morgan jumped at the chance to see his home and get to know the guys a little better. Everyone but Alexis was excited. She made lame excuses for wanting to go back to the hotel room.

"Nothing is wrong with me; I'm just tired and I was ready to go back to the hotel room and get some sleep."

"Some sleep? Are you serious?"

"Yes."

"You have been acting crazy all night. You barely said more than two words to anyone during the entire concert, and then when Malik suggests us spending some time at his house, you act like he asked us to pole dance or something."

"I'm just not into acting like a groupie."

"I don't think any of us is into acting like a groupie, Alexis," Morgan said touching up the powder on her nose.

"I can't believe that you are acting like this," Claire said angrily. "This is so unlike you. Did Massai say something to you on the way to the concert?" she asked. When she didn't answer, pretending to search for something in her purse, Claire knew she had hit the nail on the head. "What did he say? He probably told you to stop acting like you had a stick up your ass, didn't he?"

"He told me that he was interested in me, and he wished that I would give him a chance."

"I think we all wish that, Alexis," Morgan piped up.

"She's right," Claire said. "And when someone tells you he likes you, Alexis, you should be happy, not the other way around. What if he is the one, and you're walking around here acting too stuck up to find out?"

"I'm sure his girlfriend thinks he's the one for her."

"Not from what Malik says."

"What did he say?" Alexis asked, her interest rising.

"He told me that Massai's girlfriend is only with him for his money and is cheating on him."

"Why would someone as good-looking, smart and successful as Massai stay with someone like that?" she wondered.

"I didn't get that deep into his business. But if you want to know, you could always ask him yourself."

"I'm not asking him that."

"Why not? Malik says that Massai never deals with any of the women on the road and that you are the first woman he has shown any interest in since he's been with Eva."

"You know what? This is probably just some kind of game they're trying to run on me. I bet they do this all the time, and I'm not falling for it," Alexis declared, using her fingers to comb out the tangles in her hair.

"You are making up any excuse not to let yourself like Massai."

"What are you three doing in there?" Malik called from the hallway.

"We're coming," Claire replied, and then turned to Alexis and said quietly, "Stop being so stubborn and let yourself be happy, even if it is only for a couple of days."

Claire opened the door and they exited the bathroom. Two of them paired off—Morgan with Orlando and Claire with Malik, leaving Alexis standing alone in the hallway. She wandered from beautifully decorated room to beautifully decorated room and ended up in the state-of-the-art kitchen from which she could see the sparkling pool.

Leaving through the French doors, she stepped into the massive backyard and immediately smelled chlorine. At the pool's edge, Alexis kneeled down and used her fingertips to test the water's temperature. Standing again, she removed her shoes and sat on the pool's edge, submerging both pedicured feet into the cool blue water.

"Having fun?" A deep voice asked. She turned around and looked up at Massai. At six feet, seven inches and 230 pounds, Massai seemed larger than life. "I thought you would have been in the theater with everyone else," he said, taking off his own shoes and socks and sitting so close to her that their shoulders were touching. She thought she could hear his heart beating.

"Everyone was pairing off, so you know," she said quietly, as Massai lowered his long legs into the water. "Where did you disappear to?"

"I was in the game room checking my voicemail."

"Yeah, your phone rang about a hundred times while we were at the concert," Alexis observed. "Anybody interesting?"

"Just Eva wanting to know where I was and when I was coming home."

"She's very protective, isn't she?"

"Only when she feels she doesn't have the upper hand. I can't even count the number of times I've left that same message on her cell with no response. She's the type who needs to be in control. She wants to wear the pants."

"And you let her?"

"I have been for the past few months. Eva's not the same person I used to love."

"Used to love?" Alexis asked, confused.

"I used to love her, and now I'm just tolerant. I think complacent may be a better word. I'm used to coming home and having her there. I'm used to looking up in the stands during home games and seeing her face," Massai confided.

"So familiarity is enough for you?"

"I thought it was, but I'm beginning to realize that maybe I've been wrong these past few months."

"What about her has changed?"

"She's not for *us* anymore," he explained. "She's all about what I can do for her and what I can buy her."

"So why are you still with her?" Alexis wondered, hoping she was not prying too deeply into his relationship.

"I'm not a quitter; never have been. I don't know how to give up."

"Sometimes it's not about giving up but letting go and moving on for your own good," she advised.

"Is that what you did? Let go?"

"Let go of what?"

"Whoever it was that broke your heart." Massai said, taking his gaze off the water and turning it on Alexis.

"There isn't one person who broke my heart; it's just been chipped at over the years by all the bad relationships I've been in, and now there's a big crack down the middle."

"Do you think it can be fixed?"

"I'm too scared to find out."

Silence fell between them as Alexis used her feet to make waves in the water. "So what do you want to do with your life? What legacy do you want to leave?" She decided to steer the conversation away from matters of the heart.

Massai shrugged, "I want to be a husband, a father, just be happy and successful."

"I didn't hear anything about breaking any league scoring records?"

"I'm not into all that. Basketball has always been my first love, and I play because I love the game. It's great that I can make a living doing it, and if I earn some titles in the process, that's gravy. But if I don't, oh well." Massai shrugged again. "My life will still be full and I'll still be happy."

Alexis was impressed and surprised. She was under the impression that most basketball players played because of the money and fame that came with being a professional athlete, but Massai was different. He did what he did because it made him happy. She admired him for it.

"So what about you? Is teaching what fulfills you?" he asked.

It was Alexis's turn to shrug. "I do love teaching but, like you, I want to do other things, too. I wanted to fall in love, get married, have kids, you know, the whole American Dream, but I really don't think it's in the cards for me."

He laughed. "I can't give up, and you give up too easily."

"I would hardly say I give up easily."

"I would. I mean, a few bad relationships and you're ready to buy a couple of cats and lock yourself in the house."

"Massai, my last boyfriend was married with two kids at home, and I didn't even have a clue."

"And you loved him?" he asked.

"I think I was more in love with the *idea* of him. What being with him represented." Alexis paused when Massai pulled his vibrating cellphone from his pocket and checked the screen. "Eva?"

He nodded, his eyes still on the blinking blue screen.

"Aren't you going to answer that?"

He shook his head no.

"Are you leaving?" she asked.

"Is that what you want? Do you want me to go home to Eva?"

"I didn't say that."

"Then what are you saying?" he asked quietly, gently pushing Alexis's thick dark hair back from her eyes.

She didn't respond right away, turning away and looking down at the water. "If you stay, who knows what will happen? But if you go . . ." Alexis hesitated. "If you go, I'll never know."

"I'm not ready to leave," Massai quietly assured her.

10

BILLIARDS AND BEER

"So Mr. Basketball didn't come home last night?" Carlos asked, not bothering to suppress a chuckle. Eva switched the phone from one ear to the other and checked the digital clock on the stainless-steel stove: 5:06 a.m.

"No, he didn't," Eva answered, sounding agitated.

"You're losing your touch, baby," Carlos yawned. "I've been telling you that your luck is going to run out eventually. You can't have your cake and eat it, too."

"Carlos, I haven't lost anything. This is really unlike Massai, and I'm starting to get worried. Maybe something has happened and he can't get to his cellphone." Eva looked out the kitchen's window for what seemed like the millionth time.

"Ain't nothing happened to him besides some new cat," Carlos said, laughing again.

"Massai would never cheat on me." Eva saw a set of headlights moving their way up their private driveway and sighed with relief.

"Why not?" Carlos asked bluntly. "You cheat on him. You're over here in my bed more than you are in his, so what makes you think your boy isn't going out to get a little something on the side?"

"He doesn't know about us. Most of the time I'm with you, he's on the road, anyway."

"The season is over, Eva, and you were just over here yesterday afternoon."

She watched Massai steer his BMW into the garage and estimated that she had less than three minutes to get off the phone. "He doesn't know," she insisted.

"You *think* he doesn't know."

"Why are you being so difficult? What do you know? Did you call over here and tell him or something?" she asked angrily.

"I'm not that kind of guy. Of course, it would be nice if I didn't have to share you with Money Bags, but I've been waiting nine months already, and I can wait longer if I have to. You'll realize where home is," Carlos promised her confidently.

By now Massai was in the laundry room. Eva whispered a quick goodbye and quietly put the receiver back into its rest on the counter.

He came into the kitchen and tossed his car keys onto the island. He looked at Eva suspiciously. "What are you doing up? You usually don't leave the bedroom before noon."

"I haven't been to sleep yet. Where were you? I've been worried sick. You wouldn't answer your cellphone." Eva looked into a face devoid of interest and waited for a response. "Did you hear me? I asked where have you been all night?"

"Out."

"Out?" she asked, her voice rising and her hands moving to her hips. "Out where?"

"I'm going to bed, Eva," Massai said, brushing past her as she tried to block the exit.

"You are not going to bed until we talk about this!" she declared, staring at him in disbelief. She could have sworn that she smelled perfume when he walked past her, but she made herself believe that her mind was playing tricks on her. Eva refused to believe that Carlos's predictions were true.

"So now *you* want to talk?" Massai swiveled around on the steps, fire in his eyes. "What about all the times I wanted to talk to you? What about all the times you stayed out all night, and I sat up worrying about where you were and what you were doing? I never got an explanation, so why should you?"

"Massai, you're not being fair," Eva pleaded, watching his back as he continued up the stairs. "I thought you were hurt."

"Well, I'm not, so why don't you get off my back and let me get some sleep?"

Eva could not believe what she was hearing. In all the time she had been with Massai, he had never spoken to her like that. She was used to him spoiling her, catering to her every whim and treating her like a queen. She had no idea who *this* Massai was, but she intended to get to the bottom of his strange behavior, sooner rather than later. She knew that if she allowed too much time to pass, it would only be a matter of time before the world she had so carefully crafted would come crashing down around her.

"Alexis, did you hear me?" Claire asked, flipping through the New Orleans tour guide she had purchased before leaving Detroit.

"No, what did you say?" Alexis said, rolling over in bed but not removing the covers from over her head.

"I said that we should go to the Riverwalk today to do some shopping. This is our third day here, and can you believe we haven't even gone shopping?" Claire's brightly animated tone made what Alexis was about to tell her all the more difficult. "Then we can go to one of those voodoo shops. I heard they have all types of crazy stuff. Maybe we can get a little doll that looks just like Kevin and poke holes in his face," she said, laughing.

"I can't go," Alexis said, the pillow muffling her voice.

"What did you say?" Claire asked, coming over and snatching the pillow from under Alexis's head and glaring down at her.

"I said I can't go."

"Why not? Are you feeling okay?" Claire touched her palm to Alexis's forehead to check for fever.

"I feel fine; I just have other plans."

"We are not going to let you sleep all day," Morgan warned from the balcony.

"I won't be sleeping."

Claire put her hands on her hips and frowned at Alexis. "Then what are you going to be doing?"

"Well, I'm not exactly sure."

"What the hell are you talking about?" Claire said, exasperated.

"Massai is picking me up later."

Morgan came in and looked at Alexis disbelievingly. "So you have a date?"

"It's not a date."

"Then what is it, exactly?"

"A tour of the city."

"I would love to know what happened between the two of you last night. One minute you're saying that you can't stand him and the next you're going out with him. Alone."

"What did happen last night?" Morgan asked, sitting next to Alexis on the bed.

"Nothing. We just talked and got to know each other a little bit."

"Did he tell you about his girlfriend?" Claire asked excitedly.

"Yes, he did."

"Well, what did he say?"

"None of your business."

"Oh, my God, you must really like him if you're not going to tell *us* what he said!" Morgan exclaimed, smiling.

"I don't like him; we're friends."

"Friends with benefits?" Claire asked slyly.

"Nothing happened," Alexis insisted.

"Maybe not last night, but I bet something will happen before we go back to Detroit."

"I don't think so," Alexis said. "And since you two are all up in my business, what did you do last night?"

"Little Miss Committed over here got her groove on," Claire revealed, pointing at Morgan.

"Are you serious?" Alexis asked, surprised. "What happened?"

"I don't know," Morgan began, throwing her arms up in the air with a pained expression on her face. "One minute we were watching *New Jack City* and the next Malik started handing out bottles of Heineken."

"Okay," Alexis said, intrigued. "How do you go from watching *New Jack City* to having sex?"

"I honestly don't know. I don't even remember how many drinks I had. All I know is we somehow ended up butt-booty naked in the game room on top of a pool table."

"On top of the pool table?" Alexis screeched. "Oh, my God, Morgan, what the hell were you thinking? I expect something like that from Claire, but not from you."

"Excuse me?" Claire interrupted.

"I know," Morgan said, completely ignoring Claire. "Orlando was so drunk that he couldn't even remember my name. He kept calling me Brandy."

"Well, what about Craig? Are you going to tell him?" Alexis asked, finally sitting up in bed and securing an elastic band around her ponytail.

"No, I'm not going to tell him. Do I look crazy to you?"

"Crazy enough to sleep with a guy on a pool table the first time you meet him," Claire said with a smirk.

Morgan ignored Claire again and continued. "And even if I did tell Craig, what would I say? 'Baby, I had sex with a guy in New Orleans and he changed my name to Brandy?' "

"I guess you've got a point there," Alexis agreed, before turning to Claire. "So, Ms. Henry, what did you and Malik do last night?"

"Nothing as exciting as eight ball over there," Claire joked. "We kissed a little, talked. He's really not my type, though. He's way too into basketball, but he is cute and rich and fun, so I told him that we would hang out tonight *after* the concert."

"Okay, Claire, I get your point," Alexis said. "But it doesn't seem like you're all into girl time yourself, inviting Malik everywhere we go."

"I did not invite him. He offered to take us to some clubs. I thought it would be fun, considering your birthday is tomorrow. We can celebrate after the concert. And you're the one making dates without checking to see what Morgan and I have planned."

"Number one, it's not a date. Number two, I don't have to check with you, or anyone else, before I make plans. I'm grown, in case you've forgotten."

"Well, since you're so set on deserting your girls, I hope you at least get some while you're gone."

Alexis laughed and looked at her friend. "My name is not Brandy."

11

FAMILY TIES

Eva sat in the fluffy black armchair next to the California king-sized bed she shared with Massai and watched him bound around the bedroom pulling on shirts and shorts only to change his mind, starting the process all over again. He hadn't said more than a sentence to her all day, and she knew for sure that something was going on that he wasn't telling her.

"So what are your plans for the day?" Eva asked as Massai came out of his walk-in closet fastening a platinum Rolex watch around his wrist.

"Nothing much. I'll be going to some clubs with Malik and Orlando later."

"And right now?"

Massai's jaw's tightened before he answered, a sure sign that he was lying. "I have a meeting with Todd," he said, referring to the agent he had been with since graduating from Duke and entering the draft.

"You're wearing jean shorts, a T-shirt and gym shoes to a business meeting?" Eva asked, her voice tight with skepticism.

Massai placed his wallet in his back pocket. "It's casual. We're meeting at The Gumbo Shop, and then I have some running around to do." Massai checked his watch and quickly walked toward the double doors of the bedroom.

"Great, then if it's casual, I can go with you, right?" she asked, getting up and strutting over to her own walk-in closet.

"Um . . ." Massai began, his jaw's tightening again. Eva stopped and looked over her shoulder at him and saw the panic in his eyes. "Eva, I'm already running late," he said, tapping the watch's face. "It'll be a lot faster if I just go."

Eva walked over to Massai. Her hands, adorned with long acrylic nails painted a fiery red, roamed Massai's body until she reached the zipper of his shorts. "Don't you want to spend time with me anymore?" she pouted, standing on tiptoe to plant a kiss on his mouth.

Massai grabbed her hand and removed it from his genitals. "I really don't have time for this, Eva; I'm going to be late. Why don't you plan something for us to do another day?"

Massai turned and swiftly walked out of the bedroom, leaving her dazed and confused. He had never turned down her advances before. Even if they were in the middle of a heated argument, she knew that she could just touch Massai a certain way and everything would be okay. This time was different.

As soon as his footsteps faded she snatched up the phone and frantically dialed.

"Carlos Lewis."

"I think you were right. Massai is seeing someone else."

"Eva, how many times do I have to tell you not to call me at work talking about some other man?"

"I'm sorry, but it's important."

"Important to you or important to me?"

"What should I do?" she asked, ignoring Carlos's sarcasm and the annoyance in his voice.

"About what?"

"About Massai and whoever it is he's sneaking around with?"

"So now you believe me?"

"Well, this morning when he came home he smelled of perfume, and just a few minutes ago he made up some story about having a meeting with his agent just to get out of the house."

"So?"

"Are you listening to me? My man is cheating on me!" Eva yelled hysterically.

"Oh, no, boo hoo," he mocked. "The man you have been cheating on for months is finally getting a clue and stepping out on you. What the two of you need to do is stop playing these silly games and go ahead and go your separate ways. Then you can be with me exclusively."

"That was not the plan, Carlos."

"So what was the plan?"

"The plan was to get Massai to marry me," she said desperately.

"Well, what the hell am I here for? Just a little piece to tide you over while Massai is on the road?" he asked angrily.

"Of course not, baby," Eva assured Carlos, softening her voice. "You know I love you and that I'm just with Massai for one reason. As I've told you before, I'm doing this for us. Once I'm married to Massai for a while I can file for divorce and get half of everything. *We* can get half of everything."

"Have you ever heard of a little thing called a prenuptial agreement?"

"Massai is not the type to ask me to sign one of those," she told Carlos confidently.

Carlos sighed, sitting back in his leather desk chair and propping both feet on his mahogany desk. "Well, it seems like your plan may not be working, Eva."

"Now do you see my problem?"

Carlos closed his eyes and thought of his current lifestyle. As a computer engineer, he was by no means poor, but thinking about gaining millions of dollars for loaning his girl out a few nights a week was just too easy. He could see the money, and the stacks he envisioned nearly gave him a hard-on. "Yeah, that is a lot of money," he told her, trying to downplay his enthusiasm.

"I have to do something. Maybe I should confront him?" she wondered, the wheels in her head began turning wildly.

"Bad idea," he said. "Confronting him is going to put him on the defensive, and that's the last thing you want."

"Well, I don't know what else to do," Eva whined.

"I'm sure you will come up with something; you always do."

They ended their conversation, and she remained on the edge of the bed, slowly looking around at all the things she stood to lose. Holding her head in her hands, she felt a single tear trickle down her cheek. She quickly wiped it away and looked around the room again. The thick carpet and opulent décor were light years away from the place she came from.

Eva, the product of an alcoholic mother and absentee father, grew up on the south side of Chicago, poor and hungry. For breakfast, lunch and oftentimes dinner, she would eat saltine crackers and water, hoping that the combination would swell in her stomach and make her feel full. Clothing from the Goodwill and dusty, run-over shoes were staples of her wardrobe as a child. It wasn't until she turned seventeen years old that she realized that her pretty face and nearly perfect body would be her ticket out of the ghetto and to a better, brighter life.

Five days before her high-school graduation Eva moved out of her mother's apartment in the projects and into a condo on Lakeshore Drive with the forty-four-year-old man she had met while waiting tables at a Michigan Avenue restaurant. In exchange for freaky sex and home-cooked meals, Robert bought her anything her heart desired and even paid her way through nursing school.

Four years and one nursing degree later, Eva packed her bags and disappeared in the middle of the night from the apartment she shared with Robert. Her destination was New Orleans. Two weeks later, she met Massai and realized instantly that she had hit the mother lode. Now everything seemed to be falling down around her head; when she closed her eyes, she saw herself back in Chicago, dirty and eating crackers for dinner.

Eva picked up the phone again and dialed. "Hello?" A voice thick with sleep and liquor came on the line.

"Hi, Mama. How are you?"

"Well, well, well. Long time no hear from. How long has it been? Three months now? Living down there in the big mansion has you confused about who you really are." Joanna Norris started in on her daughter immediately.

"No, it's not that." Eva felt the need to explain. "I've just been really busy. You know we redecorated the house a couple of months ago."

"Isn't that nice," Joanna said with ill-concealed sarcasm and loathing.

Eva took a deep breath and plowed ahead. "Well, I called because I need some advice on a problem I'm having."

"Knocked up, huh?" Joanna coughed and, Eva guessed, probably took a long drag on a cigarette. "Better get an abortion before you're too far along. You know, once you have a baby, that man you're with will disappear; just like your daddy left us."

"No, Mama, that's not it. I'm not pregnant."

"Thank God. All kids do is give you trouble, anyway. Not worth the hassle."

Eva mentally said a prayer of thanks that she no longer had to endure her mother's daily output of negative attitudes. "I think Massai is cheating on me."

"Eva, I have told you time and time again that don't no man stay for too long. If he wants to leave, then that's exactly what he's going to do, and there is nothing you can do to stop him."

At the end of the conversation, Eva was more depressed than ever. She sat in the same spot on the bed for more than forty-five minutes, replaying the last couple of days in her head. Then something her mother had said during their brief conversation suddenly struck her as brilliant.

"Knocked up?" she had asked, immediately assuming that was the problem she was calling to discuss.

Having a baby was the perfect solution. Though she found the prospect of becoming fat unappealing, she knew that Massai was not the kind of man to shirk his responsibilities. She also knew that he wanted nothing more than to be a father, and Eva decided that she would become his fairy godmother and turn his dream into reality.

Newly inspired, she went into her huge walk-in closet and searched through one of her drawers. Poking through panties and bras, she finally located a yellow sewing kit and unsnapped the lid. Pushing aside spools of thread, scissors and a thimble she found what she was looking for. Extracting a small white envelope from the box, Eva opened the flap and chose the smallest, slimmest needle she could find.

Returning to the bedroom she kneeled in front of the nightstand on Massai's side of the bed and pulled out the drawer containing his stash of Magnum condoms. She scooped up every single one. Holding the needle firmly between her index finger and thumb, Eva began to poke tiny, undetectable holes into each condom.

At first, she was unsure whether this was something she really wanted to do. But after putting three small holes into the first condom, she rubbed her thumb over the foil packaging and felt nothing abnormal. Feeling more confident, she repeated the process until she had altered the reliability of all twenty condoms.

12

TRANSITIONS

"Where in the hell have you been?" Claire demanded as Alexis approached the table she and Morgan were sharing.

"Well, hello to you, too," Alexis answered sarcastically, tossing her purse onto the table.

"I'm serious, Alexis. I left about fifteen messages on your phone."

Alexis could tell from her tone that Claire was really upset, so wiping the smile she had worn all day off her face, she sat down on the opposite side of Morgan and softened her response. "I'm sorry, Claire, but Massai and I just lost track of time."

"You were with Massai all this time?"

"Yes. We were having such a good time we didn't notice seven o'clock had come and gone."

"You missed the concert. Do you know that Morgan and I waited almost an hour for you?" she asked, sounding seriously distressed, shooting daggers at Alexis with her eyes.

"Look, I already apologized. If my saying sorry isn't good enough, then I really don't know what else to say."

"I'll tell you what you need to be saying," Claire began with a ghetto-girl twist of her neck. "You need to say that you're going to give me back my seventy-five dollars I paid for that show."

Alexis was fed up with the testy exchange. "Fine, Claire, that's not a problem. As soon as we get back to the room, I'll write you a check."

"That's what I thought," she responded. "And it better not bounce."

"Where is Massai?" Morgan asked, changing the subject.

"He's over at the bar with Orlando and Malik," she replied, still peeved at Claire. "Aren't you two going to ask me how my date went?"

"Oh, I thought it wasn't a date."

"It wasn't." Alexis realized her slip of the tongue. "I meant how my *outing* went."

"How did it go?" Morgan asked, again trying to play peacekeeper.

"It was, hands down, the best date I've ever been on."

"There you go using that 'D' word again," Claire laughed.

"Fine! It was the best outing with a man I've ever been on."

"Where did he take you?" Morgan inquired.

"We went to Mardi Gras World, you know, where they make the floats. The work these artists put into the floats is amazing. Then we walked around the Garden District looking at the historic homes and just talking. After that we went to dinner."

"Alexis, I'm not trying to throw salt, really, but I've been places with my grandma that were more exciting," Claire said, looking unimpressed.

"Okay, so we didn't dance on any tabletops or drink ourselves into a stupor, but it was nice. We got the opportunity to really talk and get to know each other. It was so natural, and I can honestly say that there was never a lull in the conversation. I really feel as if I've known him all my life."

"Sounds to me like you're about to get caught up," Morgan said with an I-told-you-so look on her face.

"I don't think so," Alexis assured her friends. "I like Massai and I think he is a wonderful man, but he's *Eva's* wonderful man."

"Who is Eva? Is she that skank who calls herself his girlfriend?" Claire queried.

"Skank or no skank, she's still his girlfriend and I have to respect that. Not to mention the fact that I'm not getting emotionally involved with another man."

"So you're still on that trip? I thought your going on an *outing* with Massai meant that you changed your mind about all of that."

"Nothing has changed. I went out with Massai as a friend and nothing more."

"Yeah, right," Morgan said smiling. "When you were talking about him your face lit up like a damn Christmas tree."

"No, it didn't."

"Yes, it did," Claire confirmed, her smile just as wide as Morgan's.

"Well, if it did it was because it's hot in here."

"Whatever," they chimed in unison.

"And even if Massai and I did get together, it would never work. I'm on the rebound from Kevin, he has a girlfriend and we live a thousand miles away from each other. If anything, we could only realistically have a little summer fling, and it would have to end at that."

"So you've been thinking about it?" Morgan asked, her smile widening.

"No, I haven't been thinking about it, but if I had been thinking about it that's what I would think."

"You're crazy. You just said you like him and he definitely likes you, so what's the problem?" Claire asked, not understanding Alexis's dilemma.

"Was I talking to myself when I just rattled off the reasons Massai and I could never be anything more than friends? If I got involved with him it wouldn't be a question of *if* I would get hurt, but more like *when*."

"You'll never find anyone to spend the rest of your life with if you keep that attitude," Morgan said, shaking her head in pity.

"Good, then my plan is working."

"I ordered your drink," Massai said, placing an amaretto sour in front of her and pulling up a chair. He and Orlando had sneaked up behind them, causing Alexis to worry about how much he had heard.

"You know, you two really make a cute couple," Morgan observed, accepting a drink from Orlando.

"We're not a couple," Alexis said, very much aware of the smile on Massai's face.

"Thank you," he said, sitting up a little taller. "We do make a nice couple, don't we?"

"We're not a couple," Alexis insisted again.

"Don't fight it, Alexis," Massai said, causing everyone at the table except Alexis to laugh. "I'm just playing; don't be so sensitive," he said, grabbing her hand and leading her onto the jam-packed dance floor. Bodies were crushed together, forcing Massai and Alexis to press their bodies against each other.

The music thumping over the speaker nearly matched the intensity of Alexis's heartbeat. Drawing her even closer, Massai bent over and whispered in her ear, "Happy birthday."

Alexis looked at Massai's platinum-and-diamond watch and saw that the time was now 12:02; she was officially twenty-five years old. She reached up and placed her hands on both sides of his smooth face. She stood on her tiptoes and brought his ear closer to her mouth. "Thank you."

They spent the next hour and a half on the dance floor, dancing so close to each other that their bodies said things that their lips would not. Oblivious to the speed of the song, Massai held Alexis as if he never wanted or intended to let her go. And she really didn't want him to. Never in her life had she felt so comfortable so quickly with a man. It always seemed as if the getting-to-know-you phase was always awkward and filled with half-truths to get the other person to like you that much more. But the time she spent with Massai was completely different. Relaxed conversation, easy banter and an undeniable sexual attraction made the two want to spend more and more time together, despite the consequences they both felt would eventually follow.

When Massai turned Alexis around and put his hands on her hips and rubbed her body through the silk of her dress, it was all Alexis could do not to scream out loud that she wanted him. Instead, she closed her eyes, swaying back and forth to the beat and imagining the way Massai's hands, mouth and tongue would feel against her naked skin. Her back pressed against his rippling chest, causing a soft moan to escape her lips. As if sensing her pleasure and the erotic thoughts floating through her head, Massai lowered his mouth to her ear. "I want to take you back to your hotel room."

Everything for Alexis stopped in an instant. The music ceased, the partygoers on the dance floor reappeared and her eyes flew open. She wiggled out of his embrace and left him standing alone and confused on the dance floor as she headed to the club's exit. As much as she wanted Massai to do the things she had envisioned on the dance floor, she was certain going further with him would be wrong and emotionally painful in the end. Outside, Alexis rested against the brick façade of the building and pushed the hair out of her face.

"Alexis, what's wrong?"

She looked up at Massai and shook her head. "Things are moving way too fast for me, Massai."

"We were just dancing."

"Talking about having casual sex is a whole lot more than dancing."

"Who was talking about having casual sex?"

"You."

"Me?"

"I want to take you back to your hotel room," Alexis mocked in the deepest, manliest voice she could muster.

"I didn't mean casual sex, Alexis," he said chuckling at her impression of him.

"I don't understand why you're laughing, because I don't find anything funny."

"You are blowing this way out of proportion."

"I don't think so. I've known you for less than a week and already you're trying to get into my pants. If you're that horny, you need to go home to your woman."

"Alexis, I haven't even tried to kiss you yet, so why would I try to go from hand-holding to sex in a twelve-hour period?"

"Because you're a man, and all men are the same."

"Don't start that shit with me again, Alexis," he said angrily. "We were having a good time, so don't ruin it." Massai inhaled the humid Louisiana air deeply and then exhaled loudly. "Let's go back inside."

"I can't. I can't do this, Massai. It's wrong. You have a girlfriend, and I have a promise to myself and my heart to keep."

"I just want you to relax and have a good time. It's your birthday, for God's sake. Pretend I never said anything."

"I don't do this. I don't behave this way. I don't go on vacation and pick up guys, especially guys who have girl-friends. I don't normally fall for men who are otherwise occupied." Alexis buried her face into her hands.

"So you are falling for me?" he asked, going back into Alexis's personal space.

Exasperated, she removed her hands from her face and said acidly, "You're missing the point here, Massai."

"No, I'm not. You're the one missing the point, so let me speak slowly to make sure you understand. I like you and you like me. We are two grown-ass adults, so let's stop playing these middle school games and see where things go between us."

"Massai, I don't do casual sex," Alexis repeated, feeling helpless as Massai inched closer to her and ran his long fingers through her hair.

"Neither do I," he said looking into her eyes. "If and when we take that next step, I can guarantee there will be nothing casual about it." Massai put a finger under her chin, tilting it up toward his own.

Her heart pounded against her dress as he licked his lips and moved in closer. She knew she should step back and make what was happening stop. But she didn't. She knew that she should run back into the club and join her friends. But she couldn't. Her body wouldn't move. While her head told her to run, her heart and the intense tingle she felt over her entire body forced her to stay.

"You are so sure of yourself. How can you be so certain that you and I will be doing anything more than holding hands?"

"As I said, I don't know how to quit."

13

DETERMINATION

"There is absolutely no way I'm going to spend the night with you, alone, anywhere near a bed," Alexis told Massai, not believing that he had the audacity to ask her something like that. It was her last night in New Orleans, and he was insisting that she spend it with him.

"Alexis, your mind stays in the gutter. You always think somebody is trying to get you between the sheets. That is not the reason I brought this up. I was simply suggesting that we go to Malik's house, hang out, make drinks and watch some TV. And I think *I* should be the one worried about being taken advantage of because, from the sound of it, you won't be able to control yourself around me."

They both laughed at his last comment. But she knew he had a point. Ever since the kiss outside the club two days ago on her birthday, she had been able to think about little else. Her mind was filled with constant thoughts of her and Massai in various sexual positions and scenarios. His lips, tongue and hands were always on her mind, and when they were together she felt as if she could spend the entire time in his arms kissing. He was dangerous, and the thought of being alone with him for that long was both exciting and scary. She knew that he was playing a game of reverse psychology with her, and it was working. He got her to agree to spend the night with him, but she set the conditions. Alexis told him that they must sleep in separate beds, be fully dressed at all times and three drinks would be their limit. When she handed him her list of conditions, written on hotel stationary, Massai looked at her as if she had lost her mind. But she was serious, refusing to even get into the car until he had agreed to each and every one of them.

"You are being overly careful," he told her as he drove across the city to Malik's home.

"You can never be too careful."

From the second they walked into Malik's guest-house, the sexual tension between them thickened. Massai showed her around the mini-mansion, which had the same decor as the main house. The bedroom was last on the tour. Both hesitated before going inside. They looked at each other, and before he could react, Alexis bolted from the room and sped back to the living room, plopping down in front of the television.

"What do you expect to happen tonight?" she asked him as he joined on the couch, spooning up ice cream from a pint container.

"I'm just trying to spend some time with you, because I won't be seeing you for awhile," he said.

"You're not answering the question."

"What I would like to happen and what actually is going to happen are two very different things."

"I want to know both, then. What you want to happen and what you think will happen."

Massai sat quietly before answering. It was obvious that he was choosing his words very carefully before speaking. He put his spoon on the glass coffee table, replaced the top on the ice cream carton and clasped his hands. "I would like for you to let me take you into that bedroom, turn down the sheet and make you forget every other man you've ever been with."

"Massai, that can absolutely not happen," Alexis said, feeling nervous and curious at the same time.

"And I am fully aware that you are not ready for that so . . . I guess we'll just chill."

"How can you just say something like that and follow it up by, 'I guess we'll just chill'?" Alexis asked, turning to look at him.

"Because I don't want to put any pressure on you. I wouldn't have mentioned it, but you asked and I didn't want to lie. I understand and respect the fact that you're not ready to take that next step with me and that's fine. I can wait."

"What do you mean you can wait?"

"I'll wait as long as I need to, that's what I mean."

"And who says you'll get the opportunity to wait? In case you've forgotten, today is my last day here."

"Are you saying that after tonight we won't see each other again?"

"That's a possibility."

"You honestly believe that once you get on that plane that's it?" he asked, looking at her seriously.

"Why should I believe anything else?"

"Because there's something between us that you don't want to acknowledge. At least not out loud. I can't believe that you would go back to Detroit and act like we never met."

"I didn't say we wouldn't keep in touch. Of course you'll hear from me, Massai. We have a friendship, if nothing else."

"And a friendship is all that you're satisfied with?"

"Anything else wouldn't work. We would be asking for trouble," Alexis sighed.

"I want to be more than your friend, and I know deep down so do you." He took her hand in his and kissed it. "Give me a chance to show you how serious I am."

"And how am I supposed to do that with Eva calling your cellphone every five minutes and me leaving in the morning?"

"Don't leave," he responded, as if it was the easiest decision in the world. "You don't have to go back to work for a month, you could stay here and we could go from where we are right now."

"Stay here?" Alexis asked, sweeping her hand around the room. "You want me to stay here hidden in your friend's house like some sort of concubine?"

"You're not giving me enough credit. I don't want you to be my concubine. I want you to be with me, my better half."

"Massai, your math isn't adding up. Three halves do not make a whole," she said, referring to his current half, Eva.

"I don't want you to leave," he repeated.

"You don't mean that. When I get on that plane, I'll be nothing more than a girl you met and kissed outside a club once upon a time."

"If that's what you think, then don't get on that plane."

"As long as Eva's in your life, there's no place for me."

"It's not as simple as you're making it out to be."

"Oh, yes, it is. You want me to stay, but you can't let her go. You want me to play second fiddle, and I'm nobody's second fiddle."

"You're the entire band."

Alexis was softened by his last comment. "I wish we would have met a long time ago; before you met Eva and before Kevin came along and destroyed what little trust I had left in men. I think we should just consider this a good time and leave it at that."

"I want you to stay," Massai told her again, this time looking deep into her eyes. "I want to continue this."

"I can't stay here. I would be playing myself if I did."

"Well, if you won't stay then let me fly out to be with you."

"What would you tell Eva?"

"Why do you keep bringing her up?" he asked, annoyed, exasperated and befuddled.

"Your relationship with her is a reality that you aren't facing, Massai. I'm not trying to pressure you into getting rid of her; I'm trying to make you see the bigger picture. It's not smart to begin something new when you haven't finished the old."

"My relationship with Eva was finished long before I ever met you."

"If that were true, she wouldn't still be living with you. I want you to be happy, Massai, but I don't think you really know what will make you happy. You are in a bad relationship. I agree that you need to do something about it, but don't use me to get out of something that's not working."

"Are you saying that you don't want to be with me?" he asked, grabbing the remote and turning the television off.

"I'm saying that it would never work."

"You're saying that you wouldn't give it a chance to work. You're a pessimist."

"No, Massai, I'm a realist."

He looked at her for a long time but said nothing. He had never felt this way about a woman and refused to let her get away, especially without a fight. "You know people get married in a lot shorter time than we've known each other."

"Be serious."

"I am serious. There's something between us, and it's more than a sexual attraction. I really think we need to explore it and see where it takes us."

"I'm not staying."

"Then I'll book my flight to Detroit," he said, reopening the ice cream container as if the discussion was no longer up for debate.

"Massai, I don't think that's a good idea," she said softly, taking the ice cream and spoon from his hand and placing them on the coffee table next to a DVD they had rented earlier.

"That's part of your problem, Alexis," he began, kissing her cheek, then her neck, finally moving to her lips. "You think too much. You're always weighing the good and the bad when you should really just be feeling, following your heart."

"I've followed my heart before and all I've gotten in return is heartache and humiliation," she said, closing her eyes and blocking out everything except the way his mouth felt against her own. Even though she tried hard to deny it, every time he kissed her she found herself falling deeper and deeper into confusion about where their relationship was heading.

"How many times do I have to tell you that I won't hurt you? Unless, of course, you want me to," Massai said suggestively, before deepening the kiss. Alexis lost her breath and her voice as he slowly began to unbutton the black cap-sleeve blouse she was wearing. His hands moved deftly over the buttons until he exposed the bra that pushed her breasts to attention and made them appear more voluptuous than they actually were.

He pulled away from her mouth and pushed the open blouse from her shoulders, lowering his head to place sensual kisses on her collar, shoulders and, finally, cleavage. Alexis recognized that what was happening was going against everything she said she would not do, but she was barely able to contain the pleasure she felt.

She put one hand on the back of his neck and pressed his head deeper into her chest. Massai's hands moved from her waist to her back, and in one quick motion, he unhooked her bra. He leaned back and watched the black lacy undergarment come to rest around her perfectly toned midsection. Alexis watched his chest rise and fall. He looked at her and then closed his eyes, taking in a labored breath. Massai opened his eyes again and then shook his head.

"I should stop," he said, getting up off the couch and exposing his arousal.

"I don't know if I want you to," Alexis said, meaning every word. She sat on the plush suede couch feeling more exposed and vulnerable than she'd ever been; amazingly, she wanted him to continue. The voice of responsibility and sensibility she usually heard inside her head had vanished with that first kiss and was replaced by an ache between her legs that was so strong and forceful she didn't even trust herself to stand.

"You're not ready, and I don't want you to do anything that you'll regret in the morning," he told her, running his hands through his hair and centering his gaze on the front door, anything to keep himself from looking at her naked breasts.

"Massai, just come back to the couch. I'm a big girl, and I can make my own decisions."

He again shook his head. "I don't want it to be like this."

"Like what?" she asked, beginning to feel rejected.

"In my friend's house, with Eva still in my life. And who knows when or if I'll ever even see you again," he said, his voice strained.

Feeling self-conscious, Alexis refastened her bra and buttoned her shirt. Massai sat in the armchair facing her. She was in shock, and it showed all over her face. Frantically searching her memory, she couldn't remember a time when a man had turned her down the way he just had. The few men she had been intimate with in her lifetime always behaved as if she was the most beautiful and irresistible creature they had ever laid eyes on. Even though his reasons seemed sincere, she still couldn't understand why he was treating her like the newest carrier of the Ebola virus.

"I'm embarrassed," Alexis laughed nervously, wiping her sweaty palms on her light-colored jeans. "This has never happened to me before."

"Don't think I stopped because I'm not attracted to you. That couldn't be further from the truth. I've never wanted anyone more than I want you. But the problem is that I want more than sex from you. I want what we are getting ourselves into to be right for both of us, physically *and* emotionally."

It was at that moment and with those words that Alexis realized with clarity that Massai was the real thing. Any other man would have jumped all over her, caring not about the state of her heart but only about how good she could make them feel. Massai was different. He respected her mind, body and principles. Slowly but surely he was working his way into her spirit, and the more she resisted what was happening so naturally between them, the more she began to realize that she was losing the battle to protect her heart. It was, therefore, almost a relief she was leaving New Orleans the next morning. Alexis hoped that being in her own environment and returning to her daily routine would take her mind off Massai and the possibility that he could be the one she had been looking for her whole life.

14

VOICEMAIL

Alexis entered her apartment wearing a slightly bittersweet smile. Although happy to be home, she was still a bit sad. Thoughts of Massai and what might have been had occupied her thoughts the entire plane ride home. And she still wasn't sure whether the decision to leave him and come back to Detroit had been a good one. She had just about convinced herself that leaving was the only way to keep her promise to herself, but walking into an empty apartment had her second-guessing herself. Her apartment seemed so lonely—no voices, laughter or activity to make the two-bedroom space feel like a home.

She flipped the light switch by the door and the room was instantly bathed in soft fluorescent light, making the place seem a bit more alive. She cleared her throat and the sound she made echoed off the walls, startling her. Alexis sighed and felt so sad and lonely in that moment. The thought of this being her existence for the rest of her life was almost too depressing to bear.

Going into the bedroom, she sat on the bed and picked up the phone. The long stuttering dial tone indicated several voicemail messages waiting for her. She typed in her code, and an automated voice announced that twenty messages were in her box.

The first three were from telemarketers trying to sell her new health insurance, a water-filtration system and a machine that would clean the gutters she didn't have. Alexis deleted the sales pitches and moved on to a message from her sister, Alicia.

"Alexis, this is Alicia, your sister. Remember me? The bride? Anyway, I'm calling this number because it seems that while you're in New Orleans, you are refusing to answer your cellphone. At first, I thought it was just me, but I had Mommy call, too, and you didn't pick up even for her. I hope you're not down there acting all nasty when I'm here having a crisis. Anyway, I really need to talk to you about—"

Alexis laughed as her sister was cut off in mid-sentence, pressed seven for delete and waited for the next message to begin.

"Jeez, Alexis, you need to set a longer time limit for your messages. I can barely get two sentences out before the thing cuts me off. Oh, before I forget, happy belated birthday. I tried to call you on your birthday, but I just have so much going on right now. But I'm calling because—"

The service cut her off again and this time Alexis laughed even harder. This was typical Alicia. As the youngest of the siblings, she grew up spoiled and was never able to get to the point. She loved hearing the sound of her own voice, and though her intentions were good, she came across as chronically selfish.

"Good Lord, just let me spit it out before this crazy thing hangs up on me again. Okay, as maid of honor you need to get busy on my bridal shower. The wedding is only three weeks away, and if you send the invitations out now, it won't look too tacky. I can get one of the other bridesmaids to help out . . . just call me so that—"

Wiping the tears of laughter from her eyes, Alexis sighed and deleted the message. She had planned to spend the rest of her summer vacation relaxing and preparing herself for the upcoming school year, but it seemed her sister had made other plans for her time off.

"Hello, Alexis, this is Kevin. I tried to call your cellphone to wish you a happy birthday, but you didn't answer. I need to see you. I miss you. Call me when you get back into town."

With a roll of her eyes, Alexis immediately deleted his message.

"This is Alicia again. When in the world are you coming home? You need to be here to help with this wedding. Did you get your shoes? I left them on hold for you. Call me as soon as you get this message because we have to coordinate—"

Alicia had always been a little dramatic and nervous, but since she began planning her wedding nine months ago, with the assistance of her fiancé's parents' checkbook, she had become ridiculously hard to deal with.

"Ms. Hunter, this is Mrs. Garner. I hope your vacation is going well and that you are resting up for the start of a new school year. We will begin teacher training one week early, on August 25, because school will begin after

Labor Day. Please be here on the fifteenth bright and early at eight a.m. Dress is casual and comfortable. If you have any questions, you can call me at home. If not, I'll see you on the twenty-fifth."

Mrs. Garner was Alexis's principal and mentor. At forty-five years old, Elizabeth Garner reminded Alexis of a teapot, short and stout but always stylish. Her salt-and-pepper hair, which she wore in a shoulder-length bob, always looked freshly styled by the salon, and Alexis couldn't remember seeing Mrs. Garner in the same suit twice. She had taken Alexis under her wing and showed her the ropes when she started working at Discovery Academy three years ago. In return, Alexis strived to be the most dedicated and effective teacher in the school.

There were several messages from friends, one each from her mother and brother and one from a co-worker—and another from Kevin.

"Alexis, I'm leaving Kim. Filing for divorce, and I've already broken it off with Jessica. I know what I did was wrong, but I'm trying to make things right between us. I would love to talk to you about our relationship face to face."

It seemed that Kevin was not going to give up, and while annoyed he kept calling, she found it comical that he called what they had a relationship when it would be better classified as an exercise in deception. She forcefully pressed seven to delete and seriously considered changing both her cell and home numbers to keep Kevin at bay.

"This is Massai . . . I was just wondering if you got home safely." When he paused, Alexis exhaled slowly, not even realizing that she had been holding her breath from the moment she heard his voice.

"I miss you already. I know it's hard to believe, but I do. I hope this wasn't just some short-term vacation thing for you, because it wasn't for me. You're special; different from any woman I've ever known." He paused again and then added, "Call me."

She played the message three more times, enjoying the sound of his voice. Then she activated the save feature, storing his message in the voicemail's memory. After regaining her composure, she began sorting the dirty clothes from her suitcase, simultaneously dialing her little sister's phone number.

"Alicia, I'm back," Alexis said, as she took clothes from the piles in the middle of her bedroom floor to the washing machine hidden in a small alcove off the kitchen.

"Where in the world have you been? I thought you were only staying for three days?"

"We decided to stay a day longer and hang out in the city after the concerts were over. I could have sworn I told you that," she said, adding bleach to the load of whites.

"I would have remembered something like that. Did you get my messages?"

"Yes, I did. All one hundred of them," Alexis replied sarcastically.

"You really need to do something about that service. It would cut me off after about ten seconds."

"It's set for two minutes."

"I seriously doubt that. Anyway, how soon can you get over here?" Alicia asked, referring to their parents' home. "We need to talk about the shower and get these invitations sent out a.s.a.p."

"Alicia, please . . . I got home less than an hour ago and I'm tired. Can't this wait until tomorrow?"

"No, it can't. This is really important."

"Well, I'm sorry but it's going to have to wait. As I said, I'm tired . . . and also hungry. I just want to relax."

"Alexis, what if this was your wedding?" Alicia whined.

Alexis laughed lightly. "I seriously doubt there will ever be a wedding in my future."

"What are you talking about? What about Kevin? I think he is definitely marriage material."

"That's the problem. He is already in a marriage that he failed to tell me about."

"He was married? Had me fooled!"

"Well, just imagine how I feel."

"Wait a minute," Alicia began, her voice rising a few octaves. "Does this mean that you don't have a date for the wedding? You are listed for two and this is costing one hundred and fifty dollars a plate!"

"I tell you the man that I've been seeing for six months is married, and all you can think about is your precious little reception?"

"You just don't understand how much this thing is costing Eric's family. If it's any consolation, I'll find some time to do these invitations myself, okay?"

"Well, isn't that nice? And don't try to play me like I'm stupid, I know that Eric's parents are rolling in dough and were more than happy to take the burden of paying for this wedding off Mama and Daddy," Alexis said, once again sarcastic.

"Just because his parents are wealthy does not mean that I can waste money on this wedding because you can't keep a man. Just remember to pick up your shoes before they sell them to someone else. And please try to get over here tomorrow so we can talk about the shower."

"I'll be there," she assured her sister, her tone melodic.

"How was your trip? I've always wanted to go to New Orleans," Alicia said.

"It was great. A lot of fun," she answered, purposely leaving out the fact that she had met someone while down there.

"Good. And now that you've gotten all that out of your system, you can concentrate on what's really important here: my wedding."

On that note, Alexis hung up on her sister faster than the voicemail had. She found herself laughing and realized she was in a much better mood than she had been when she arrived. She decided to call Massai and let him know that she was home.

15

GUILT

"Oh, Alexis, thank you so much," Alicia gushed, engulfing her sister in a bear hug. "I can't believe you pulled it off so quickly."

Alexis smiled at her sister and sat on a wooden stool in her mother's kitchen. She slipped her cream-colored sling backs off, let them fall to the linoleum floor and began rubbing her aching feet.

"She's right, that was an amazing bridal shower," Claire agreed, entering the kitchen and putting an empty platter into the sink.

It had been two weeks since Alexis had returned from New Orleans, and planning Alicia's bridal shower had consumed all her time. She realized shortly after their telephone conversation that even though her sister was being a bit bossy and demanding, she nonetheless had a valid point. The two had always been close, and if the tables were turned, she would have been heartbroken if Alicia had taken a nonchalant attitude toward the planning of *her* wedding.

"I loved the tea-party theme," Morgan added, sitting next to Alexis. "Those little sandwiches and the cookies . . . it was really beautiful."

"I can't believe you went all out like that. Now you're not going to have any ideas left when it's time for you and Massai to walk down the aisle," Claire laughed.

"Who's Massai?" Alexis's Aunt Shara and her mother, Dana, asked at the same time. The two looked more like twin sisters than siblings five years apart. They had the same copper skin tone, hazel eyes and dark, curly hair streaked with silver.

Alexis shot Claire the most evil look she could dredge up. "Nobody."

"Well, he must be somebody or you wouldn't be looking at her like that," her mother said, closing the trash compactor under the counter.

"You look like you want to scratch her eyes out," Shara added. "So who is he?"

"This guy . . . nobody, really. I met him while we were down in New Orleans."

"You didn't tell me!" Alicia said, rejoining the conversation after having said good-bye to the rest of the bridal party. She stood in front of her sister, hands on her hips and a pout on her mouth; she hated being left out of the loop.

"I didn't say anything because it's not a big deal."

"What does he do?" her mother asked, loading party platters into the dishwasher. Dana was the kind of woman who could work without ever taking a break.

"He's in the NBA," Morgan blurted out before Alexis had a chance to stop her.

"Don't get involved with him. Those professional athletes go from woman to woman, and when they do finally decide to settle down they still have a little something on the side," Alicia warned, talking as if she had decades of dating experience under her belt. She always wanted to come off as older and more mature than her twenty years of age.

"I never said I was getting involved with Massai, and I certainly don't remember asking anyone for her opinion. He's a friend and that's all. I would appreciate it if we could drop the conversation altogether," she said, balancing first on one foot and then the other to slip her shoes back on.

"Why don't you invite him to the wedding, Alexis?" Dana suggested. "It wouldn't be any trouble. We do have that extra place, after all."

"I said we are just friends!" she retorted loudly.

"You don't talk to someone who is just a friend three times a day, Alexis," Claire interrupted.

"For everyone's information, I do not talk to Massai three times a day."

"Okay, four."

"Urgh!" she said, completely frustrated. She snatched her purse off the counter and took two long strides to the kitchen side door of the house. "I can't understand why I've become the topic of conversation here."

"We didn't mean to upset you, Alexis, but we are concerned about you. We only want you to be happy, honey," her mother said.

"I am happy, and I would be even happier if people would just trust me and stay out of my personal business."

"Massai?" Alexis said after hearing his deep voice on the other end of the phone.

"Hey, baby," he whispered. "Hold on for a second."

She waited patiently in her bathtub filled with bubbles while Massai moved from the family room to the privacy of his office. She was used to this; the whispering and late-night phone calls had become the norm since her return to Detroit, and even though she didn't like it she understood completely.

"How are you?" Massai asked after about a minute and a half.

"I'm okay, but kind of tired. Alicia's bridal shower was today."

"That's right. How did it go?"

"It turned out really nice, and Alicia was happy. That's really all that matters," Alexis sighed, her voice a bit strained.

"You sound like something is bothering you."

"You know how family can be sometimes?"

"No, I don't know. Why don't you tell me?"

Alexis allowed her body to relax in the bath, the lavender oil she added to the warm water calming her frayed nerves. "Claire mentioned you in front of my sister, aunt and mother."

"And why is that a problem?" he asked, laughing slightly.

"Because now they think we're in a relationship. I've already told you about how I'm the only one who hasn't settled down and started a family."

"I still don't see an issue, Alexis."

"They wanted me to invite you to my sister's wedding," she said, hoping he would understand how much her family's expectations bothered her.

"So are you?"

"Am I what?" she wondered, momentarily confused.

"Are you going to invite me to your sister's wedding?"

"Do you want me to?"

"I want to see you, and I do have a tux . . ."

She hesitated for a second, seriously considering asking Massai to come to the wedding next week. She could imagine him twirling her around on the dance floor, all the guests watching . . . and the questions from family members . . .

"No," she finally answered after replaying the scenario in her head.

"No? Just like that, huh?"

"It'll cause too many problems. Everyone will want to know who you are, what you do, where we met and if our relationship is serious or not. I really don't want to take the focus off my sister."

"You know what Alexis? You come up with one excuse after another. The problem is, as I've said before, you're just scared to let yourself be happy."

"That's not it, Massai."

"Yes it is, and it's getting really old as far as I'm concerned. You know what would happen if I came there, and it scares you to death," he said, his voice rising in frustration.

"You better keep your voice down. What would you do if Eva heard you talking to me?"

He sighed. He knew that he had been beaten. "If I got rid of her, broke it off, would you come to New Orleans then?"

"I don't know. I do want to see you, but—"

"Why is there always a 'but' with you? Why are you always second-guessing the things you want?"

"Massai, we've been through this before."

"And you still refuse to admit that you want me just as much as I want you. I'm getting tired of these games, and if you keep this up I'm going to leave you alone."

Alexis was speechless. He was always so caring and understanding but this outburst underscored the fact that she had some heavy-duty decisions to make.

"Look, I've got to go," he said quietly, the tension in his voice betraying the pain he was feeling.

"Massai, let's talk about this?" she pleaded, feeling as if she was in danger of losing the most special person in her life.

"I'm tired of talking about it Alexis, especially when you keep telling me the same things over and over. I don't think you understand that I WANT YOU and I want you to want me. But I refuse to keep begging and pouring my heart out to you when all you do is shut me down and make me feel like an asshole. I would break up with Eva, sell my house and buy out my contract so that I could be picked up by the Detroit Pistons if you wanted me to, but you won't tell me what you want one way or the other. I don't like to be strung along."

"Massai, please—"

"I'll call you tomorrow."

Alexis sat in the bathtub until the water had turned cold and the candles had burned low, upset and distracted by her exchange with Massai. She wasn't exactly sure what she was feeling, but she knew it was very far from happiness. When Massai ended their conversation as he had, her heart began to ache and tears cascaded down her cheeks. Her reaction surprised and confused her, the tears making her realize that her feelings for Massai went a lot deeper than she had admitted to herself.

She knew Massai was special, a one-in-a-million kind of man. Alexis thought back to the night before she left New Orleans when she had concluded that he was what she had always been looking for. She had left the next morning confused, had arrived back in Detroit confused and now, two weeks later, her confusion and persistent indecision were costing her the possibility of happiness.

Leaving the cold bath, Alexis wrapped herself in a towel and lay in bed staring at the wall for the longest time. Sleep refused to come, and the hours passed like seconds, but when her phone rang close to two in the morning, a smile lit up her face, her heart began to flutter and relief swept over her. Without checking the caller ID, Alexis snatched up the phone.

"I'm so glad you called back," she said eagerly.

"I'm glad that you're glad."

It took Alexis a couple of seconds to realize that the voice on the other end was not Massai's. After recognizing Kevin's voice she started to hang up; her finger was already on the end button when she decided against it. Alexis became curious to hear what Kevin had to say.

"I thought you were someone else," she said harshly, wanting to put him in his place from the very beginning. She didn't want him thinking that she actually wanted to hear from him after all he had done to her.

"So does that mean you aren't happy that I called?"

"What do you think?" she responded snippily.

"Did you get my messages?" he asked, ignoring her last comment. He remembered how difficult she could be at times.

"I did, and frankly I can't understand for the life of me why you are still trying to contact me. I thought I made it perfectly clear the last time you were here: We are over."

"I thought you may have a change of heart after hearing that I filed for divorce."

Alexis laughed contemptuously. "Kevin, absolutely nothing you can say will change my mind."

"Can we talk face to face? I feel like I still have a lot of explaining to do, and this over-the-phone thing is not working for me. Pick a day and I'll come by your place."

"You really must be crazy if you think I'm going to let you come over here!"

"Okay, then you choose a place; wherever you suggest, I'll be there."

She thought about what he was asking. She was intrigued, curious to hear what his explanation could possibly be. She knew curiosity killed the cat, but hers was getting the better of her so she agreed to meet him.

"We can meet for brunch next Tuesday. I hope that will work for you because any other day next week will be impossible because of my sister's wedding and all the stuff that goes along with that; eleven a.m., Sweet Georgia Brown."

When Alexis hung up the phone, a strange feeling came over her. She wasn't doing anything wrong, and she wasn't even in a relationship with Massai, so why did she feel as if she was being unfaithful to him?

16

THE "L" WORD

In the three days since Massai had last talked to Alexis he had picked up the phone five or six times a day intending to call her, but would always replace the receiver and end up staring at the phone. Upon ending their conversation that night, he had vowed that it would be the last time he would talk to her as long as he lived. He did not like wearing his heart on his sleeve, and it seemed that ever since he and Alexis met, that was all he had been doing. But as the minutes turned into hours and the hours turned into days, he came to realize that without Alexis in his life it felt like something was missing.

In the month they had known each other, she had somehow gotten to him. He found himself daydreaming about her, envisioning their wedding day, the birth of their first, second and third child and all the other milestones and memorable times that couples share. This feeling was new to him; Massai couldn't remember one occasion where he had found himself dreaming about a future with Eva.

Unable to deal with these feelings alone, Massai decided to drive to Malik's to get some of the thoughts constantly running through his head off his chest.

"What are you doing here?" Malik asked, stepping back and allowing Massai to enter the foyer.

"I need to talk to you."

"Well, you could have called first. I've got somebody on the way over here."

"It'll only take a minute," he assured him.

Malik closed the front door, staring at Massai as if his friend had lost his mind. "Make it quick."

"I love her," Massai blurted out before he lost his nerve.

"Who?"

"Alexis, who else?"

"You're crazy," Malik said, turning around and heading for the kitchen. "You cannot be in love with someone you just met a month ago."

"Why not? It happens all the time."

"Yeah, to insane people. You *think* you're in love, but it's just lust," he announced knowingly.

"We haven't even had sex, so how can it be lust?"

"Wait a minute," Malik said, closing the refrigerator and handing Massai a cold Heineken. "Didn't you two spend the night in the guesthouse the night before she left?"

"Nothing happened," he said simply, not wanting to get into specific details.

"You really are crazy!"

"Do you think I should tell her?" he asked, opening the bottle and letting the beer cool his throat.

"Does she love you?" Malik wondered, still not believing he was actually having this conversation.

"I don't know. She's so scared; she has a hard time telling me anything or trusting me."

"Can you blame her with Eva still living in your house, eating your food and spending your money?"

"I told her that if she would just let me know something, I would take care of that situation."

"You need to handle that situation no matter what Alexis says to you."

"I yelled at her a few days ago. Basically hung up in her face and haven't called her back since," he revealed, taking another sip of his beer. "I have to call her back, though; it feels like half of me is gone when I don't talk to her."

"You're talking like you're going to going to ask her to marry you or something," Malik said, staring at Massai and almost daring him to confirm.

"I might. I really think that this girl is it for me."

"You have gone completely insane. I'm almost scared to find out what you'll be saying after you get the panties."

He left when Malik's guest arrived with an overnight bag and a smile. During the entire twenty-minute drive back to his house, Massai rehearsed what he wanted to say to Alexis when he called her. After checking to make sure Eva was sound asleep, he went to his office and let his fingers fly over her phone number.

"Long time no hear from," she said, answering the phone after the second ring.

"How did you know it was me?" he asked, smiling at the sound of her voice.

"Caller ID."

"Were you sleeping?"

"I haven't really been able to sleep since the last time we spoke," Alexis admitted sadly.

"I'm sorry I didn't call back when I said I would."

"It's okay, Massai. You don't have any obligation to me."

He took a deep breath, wanting nothing more than to have his arms wrapped around her waist and his face buried in her hair at that very moment. "Alexis I . . . I . . . I miss you and I'm sorry for talking to you the way I did." His intentions were to tell her he loved her, but something stopped him.

"I miss you, too," she sniffled. He could tell she was crying. "And I'm sorry for lying to you."

"Lying to me?"

"About being scared. I am scared about what's going on between us."

"I want you to know that there is absolutely nothing to be scared of. I would never do anything to hurt you."

"But Massai, I can't go further with you knowing that you are still involved with Eva. It really wouldn't be fair to anyone. If you are serious about being with me, then you need to make some decisions."

"I want to see you."

"Not until you handle your business at home," Alexis said.

"Consider it handled," he said confidently.

"Don't make promises you can't keep, Massai."

"You just don't know how I feel about you."

"Well, I hope you will be in the position soon to let me know."

Eva slowly replaced the receiver and felt angry heat escaping from every orifice in her body. She couldn't believe what she had just heard while eavesdropping on one of Massai's frequent, secret and very late-night conversations.

While holding the mute button for over an hour, she had listened to him apologizing to, and then practically professing his love for, this woman he had obviously been seeing and communicating with for some time. With that single conversation, all of Eva's fears became reality; she was losing her man. Actually, from the sound of it, he was already gone and letting her know it was over was just a formality. He had spoken to Alexis with such emotion in his voice; it made her realize that this woman wasn't just some groupie, nor was their relationship a short-term fling. His feelings for her were real, and it seemed that he was using every available opportunity to let her know just how much she meant to him.

It was difficult for her to pinpoint the exact moment when he had begun seeing Alexis, but she estimated it to be about a month ago when he began acting distant and withdrawn around her. She couldn't quite understand how he had fallen for this woman so fast. By nature Massai wasn't spontaneous; it had taken months before he even showed any remote interest in Eva as more than a friend.

Eva sat on her side of the bed wondering what Alexis looked like and what was so special about her that made Massai want to give up everything he had with her. Again, she considered confronting him and asking him all the questions she so desperately wanted answers to.

She looked over her shoulder at the drawer containing Massai's condoms. It had been a month since she had compromised their effectiveness, and she was no closer to becoming pregnant than she would be if she had swallowed fifty birth-control pills at once. Despite her advances, night after night Massai refused to sleep with her. Always giving the excuse of being tired or having a headache, he had succeeded in staying as far away from Eva as possible.

Hurrying from of the bedroom and down the hall, she opened the door to his office and sidled up to his desk. "Massai, why don't you come to bed?"

"I've got some work to do. I'll be up in a little while."

She walked around his desk and began massaging his shoulders. Something he used to beg for a few months ago now seemed to disgust him; she could feel his muscles tensing up.

"You've been working nonstop for the past month. There can't be that many shoe deals in the world," she said, waiting for Massai to respond. Instead, he removed her hands from his shoulders and booted up his computer.

"I can't remember the last time we made love," she said quietly, sitting on the edge of his desk.

Again, he had no comment, but wordlessly typed in his computer's password.

"Who is she?" Eva asked, standing up and looking him square in the eyes.

"Shouldn't I be the one asking who it is you've been seeing?" he spat, anger and hatred spreading across his face with lightening speed.

"I'm going to bed," she retorted, getting up and heading for the door.

"I thought that's what you would say."

She paused at the door with her hand on the knob. "I love you, Massai."

"Do you? Or did you really mean to say you love my money?"

"How could you say that?" she said, going into actress mode.

"You're not answering the question," he said, unmoved.

"I shouldn't have to. If I didn't love you then why would I put up with being so lonely while you're on the road doing God only knows what?"

"I got the impression from the monthly credit-card bills that all the clothes and shoes you constantly buy were keeping you company."

"Why does everything keep coming back to money? I really don't see a problem. It's not like we can't afford it."

"One of us can't afford it, and I'm the only one working, so the guilty party must be you."

"So it's like that now?" Eva asked, struggling to keep her voice soft and controlled.

"I'm tired of giving you everything and getting nothing in return. Something has to change," Massai said quietly.

Eva left his office shortly after that; clearly, she was no longer in control. Her relationship and means of support were both slipping away at a runaway pace, and drastic measures would have to be taken if she was to regain the upper hand.

17

LET THE DOORKNOB HIT YOU

"I'm supposed to be meeting someone," Alexis told the hostess at Sweet Georgia Brown.

"Are you Mr. Washington's guest?" she asked, checking the reservation list.

"Yes, that's right. Has he arrived?"

"A few minutes ago," she smiled. "Right this way."

The hostess led Alexis directly to Kevin's table; he saw her striding toward him and quickly straightened his tie and stood up to greet her.

"You look beautiful," Kevin said. He attempted to kiss Alexis on her cheek, but she deftly averted her head.

"Thank you," she responded, not returning the compliment. Even though he did look amazing in his navy blue suit, pink shirt and navy-and-pink striped tie. But she refused to give him any hope that she was still attracted to him.

"I ordered a mimosa for you. I hope that's okay?" Kevin said, gesturing at the orange juice and champagne concoction that was waiting for her.

"That's fine. I don't plan to be here long enough to eat a full meal."

Kevin looked a little deflated but immediately regained his stride. "Well, I guess I'll have to make this fast," he said, folding his hands and placing them on the table. "I just wanted to let you know that it's over between my wife and me. I filed for divorce a couple of weeks ago and I've moved out, rented an apartment not too far from here."

Alexis lifted her eyebrows but remained silent, giving him the opportunity to finish.

"I want us to start over again. This time we'll put everything out on the table. I've given up everything for you, for us, and I want you to give me another chance."

"First of all, I never asked you to divorce your wife or leave your mistress for me. Second of all, there is no way in the world I would ever take you back," she informed him, crossing her arms with finality across her chest.

"We had some good times, Alexis, and just think about all I could give you."

She laughed and shook her head, "Yes, Kevin, we did have some good times, but if you really think about it all those times were lies. I don't even know the *real* Kevin Washington."

"Use this as the opportunity to get to know the real me. I promise that you won't be disappointed."

"Are you saying you want to date me?"

"That's exactly what I'm saying."

"That's impossible," she said, sitting back and slowly sipping her mimosa.

"Why?" he asked, frustration and a deflated ego written all over his face.

"I'm seeing someone. *I* am not the type to get involved with two people at the same time."

"You're seeing someone? How can you be seeing someone when we just broke up a month ago?" Kevin said, sounding irate.

"Lower your voice, Kevin. People are beginning to stare."

"I'm sorry," he said, taking a breath to regain his composure. "I'm just really confused here."

"What is there to be confused about? You are married, you have two kids and now *you're* angry because I've moved on? You've got to be joking."

"I just don't understand how you could meet someone so fast."

"Things happen, and when it's right . . . it's right."

"Alexis, that is exactly how I feel about you. We are definitely right for each other."

"You're delusional, Kevin."

"So who is this guy? I know he can't take care of you like I can," he said, playing the money card.

"Kevin, I am quite capable of taking care of myself."

"Oh, I don't doubt that. But a woman like you should only work if she wants to, and the man that she is with should be in the position to provide for her."

"I'm not for sale."

"So basically what you're trying to tell me is that he's broke?" he asked, chuckling.

Alexis reached for her purse and stood, preparing to leave. "I am so glad I found out about you before things went any further between us. You are definitely not the man I thought you were."

Ninety-nine percent effective is what the back of the pink and white box promised. Eva had never trusted these home-pregnancy tests and, even though she had never been steered wrong by one, she was still skeptical. As a nurse, she knew that the blood tests given in hospitals and doctor's offices were a bit more reliable than peeing on a stick.

Another minute ticked by and she silently prayed that she was finally getting the outcome she wanted. With trembling hands, she lifted the digital stick from the counter, sent one last prayer up to God and slowly looked at the stick. New and improved pregnancy tests were straight to the point; gone were the days of trying to decipher fading pink and blue lines. This type of test was clear, accurate and completely unmistakable. She was not pregnant.

Though both disappointed and angry, Eva was not surprised by the negative result shown on the test stick. Massai wouldn't lay so much as a finger on her, and when she was with Carlos they used condoms faithfully. She angrily tossed the stick across the immaculate bathroom and nearly screamed out in frustration. She was running out of time, options and ideas.

"Eva!" he called from the bathroom door, making her pull herself together—if only for a little while. She quickly got down on all fours, looking for the discarded test. She scooped up the packaging and stuffed everything into the very back of her personal drawer.

Eva exited the bathroom and her mouth immediately dropped open in shock. Massai's Louis Vuitton duffle bags were open on the bed and overflowing with clothes, shoes and toiletries. She clearly remembered checking his travel schedule, always on the refrigerator, earlier in the week and couldn't remember him having any trips scheduled.

"Going somewhere? she asked, crossing her arms and leaning against the armoire, trying to appear more calm, collected and in control than she really was.

"That's what I wanted to talk to you about," he said, closing both duffle bags before turning to face her.

"I'm listening."

"I've met someone," he said simply, looking her directly in the eye to gauge her reaction.

"I knew it," she said, laughing bitterly.

"I'm in love with her."

"So just forget about me, huh?"

"Our relationship has been over for months, Eva."

"I don't think that's true, Massai. Every couple has problems, and we just need to take the time to work them out."

"I'll be gone for four days, and I want you gone by the time I get back," he informed her, slinging the bags over his shoulder.

"Are you serious?" she shrieked.

"Completely serious. I've had enough and I deserve to be happy, to be with someone who wants to be with me, not for what I can *do* for her."

"And you're so sure this woman is in it for love?"

"I'm sure you're not, and right now that's all I need to know."

"Massai, what am I supposed to do? Where am I supposed to go?"

"Why don't you stay with the guy you've been sleeping with for the past six months?"

The blunt comment nearly threw Eva, but she quickly recovered. "There is no guy I'm seeing, there's only you. There has always been only you," she asserted confidently.

"You may think I'm stupid, but I'm not. I don't know his name, but I know he exists."

"That's not true, Massai," she disagreed, her voice desperate.

"Stop lying. It's over. Done. I'm leaving, and I don't want you here when I come back."

Eva stared at his retreating figure and then at the empty hall. The birds had stopped chirping outside the window and the sun was setting, a pink and orange haze coloring the sky. It had finally happened. She was going to lose everything she had worked so hard to earn. She conceded that *earn* may have been a bit of a stretch, but the word was actually accurate. It took work to lie, connive and manipulate day after day without slipping up and getting caught.

Massai was right; she really didn't love him and never had. He was just a gateway to a life that she had always wanted. Even though she knew he wasn't her type, she couldn't pass up such a chance. Eva had come to have a certain fondness for him; she thought he was adorable, funny, smart, athletic and kind, but he just wasn't her cup of tea. She liked someone rougher, a bad boy who made it perfectly clear that *she* was lucky to be with him, not the other way around. She felt that he was weak, passive and easily manipulated, and those flaws made it very easy for her to get everything she wanted out of him, no matter what the cost.

She glanced at the phone, debating whether she should call Carlos. She sensed lately that he was tiring of her schemes and problems with Massai, so she decided against confiding in him for now.

Eva looked around the room and noticed that someone, either Massai or the twice-weekly cleaning lady, had brought out her tan Gucci luggage from her walk-in closet and placed each piece neatly by the door. The suitcases, trolley and garment bag had cost around fifteen thousand dollars. The very same items that had given her so much joy the day she had purchased them were now mocking her.

"Aahh!" Eva screamed, running over to the leather bags and kicking them, hurting her right foot in the process.

With white-hot pain shooting through her foot and up to her leg, she limped back to the bed and collapsed on Massai's pillow. She honestly couldn't believe or completely grasp what was happening, but knew she had only three days to concoct something so mind-blowing that he would have no choice but to get down on his knees and ask for her forgiveness for being stupid enough to leave her.

Her heart began to palpitate when she noticed that the top drawer of Massai's nightstand was partly open. She leaned over and opened the drawer wider and gasped. The condoms that she had poked holes into were missing—all of them gone. She felt around in the drawer behind a hand towel and lubricants but came up empty. Rushing to the wastebasket in the corner near the dresser, she became more panicked when she saw that the crisp, new trash bag was free of trash and condoms.

"Damn it!" she yelled at the top of her lungs, feeling the sting of her salty tears on her cheek.

Her plan was about to backfire in a way that she never imagined. If Massai used those condoms with Alexis, then there was a good chance that she would get pregnant and Eva would be left feeling like a bigger fool for having caused it.

18

WITH THIS RING

Alexis felt relieved. Though the ceremony had been one of the most beautiful and emotional she had ever witnessed, she was glad that it was over and the reception at the Roostertail well underway. Of course she was happy for her sister, but during the ceremony she had felt the slightest twinge of jealously as Alicia and her about-to-be husband, Eric, stood in front of God, friends and family to exchange their vows. Alexis stood to the left of Alicia and held the bridal bouquet while Eric slipped the gold and diamond ring on her sister's finger and pledged to love, honor and care for her for all the days of his life. As her mother was dabbing at her moist eyes, and she felt her own eyes misting up, though not for the same reason as her mother. She knew that her mother was crying because her youngest child was getting married. She reached for the tissue she had cleverly hidden in her bouquet when the grim truth hit her: her sister's ceremony was probably something she would never experience. Although she had decided to finally let down her guard and give whatever she had with Massai a try, she shied away from thinking it would lead to marriage.

Alexis ambled over to the window and looked out at the Detroit River. The Roostertail, a nightclub in years past, was now the premier spot for wedding receptions, banquets and other important events. The venue offered gorgeous views from any angle. She looked over at Belle Isle Park with fond memories of playing there as a child.

"Look at your Uncle Moe over there trying to feel on that lady," Claire said, joining her at the window. "Somebody needs to tell him that just because the bar is free does not mean he has to drink himself into a stupor."

She looked over her shoulder and laughed at the sight of her uncle trying to coax a guest onto the dance floor, tripping over air in the process and crashing into a nearby table. "You know how he is," she said turning back to the view. "He sweats Wild Irish Rose."

They stood in silence for a minute, and then Claire asked, "What do you think about my date?"

"He's cute, but a little bit short for you."

"I know he's only five feet, nine inches, but that's taller than me, and he's pretty much a good guy. Not long-term material, but a good guy."

"Aren't you ever going to settle down?" Alexis asked, turning around to watch her sister and Eric dance to Brian McKnight on the dimly lit dance floor.

"Why should I? I'm having a great time just dating and playing the field. Maybe in about five years I'll consider doing the whole marriage and kids thing, but until then I am going to keep doing what I'm doing."

"Aren't you worried about getting old and being alone?"

"No, I'm not. Are you?" Claire asked Alexis, really wanting an honest answer.

"Yup, all the time."

"Your situation is self-inflicted, Alexis. You have someone who would do anything to be with you, and you keep blowing him off."

"I do not keep blowing Massai off. In fact, just the other day we talked and I told him that I was ready to explore what we have but not until he breaks it off with Eva. I refuse to be the other woman."

"He'll tell her to bounce."

"He hasn't yet."

"He will," Claire assured her. "I think you two are meant for each other."

"Please. I don't believe in any of that crap anymore. Love at first sight, soulmates and all that. Those ideas were developed just to sell more Valentine's Day cards."

"You used to love all that stuff—Valentine's Day, roses, those sappy-ass movies . . ."

"Yeah, but people change."

Reeva, the wedding planner, hurried toward them. "Ladies, it's time for the bridesmaids to pull the fortunes out of the wedding cake," she said in a bright voice that was becoming a bit annoying after six months of hearing it.

"Not this shit," Alexis said bitterly after Reeva left to collect the rest of the bridal party. "The last thing I need is some two-dollar charm telling me I need a hysterectomy."

"It's supposed to be only good fortunes."

"I don't have good luck," she said, reluctantly making her way over to the cake, her friend on her heels.

"Stop being so cynical. I'll wait right over here for you," Claire said, pointing to a corner seat next to Morgan.

She pulled up her pale-blue strapless Ramona Keeva maid of honor gown before it slipped any further and exposed her breast to the guests. She cursed Alicia under her breath for making her wear this while all the other members of the bridal party were fortunate enough to have straps on their gowns.

Reeva led a slightly frowning Alexis to the three-tiered wedding cake and handed her a ribbon matching the shade of her dress. Alicia's attendants were giggling with anticipation; Alexis was thinking it was the dumbest thing she had ever taken part in.

"Alexis," Morgan said in a stage whisper from the corner, "smile! You look ridiculous standing up there like you have to take a shit!"

"I feel ridiculous. This whole thing is ridiculous."

"Shh!" admonished one of the excited bridesmaids standing closest her.

She was getting ready to give her the finger, but Alicia grabbed the microphone and began instructing her attendants.

"Each bridesmaid will pull their ribbon and will receive a charm that will tell her future. All the fortunes are good ones, because I want each and every one of you to end up just as happy as I am," Alicia gushed. "Now on the count of three, ladies: one . . . two . . . three!"

The five other women in blue silk snatched their ribbons out of the cake as if their lives depended on it, while Alexis yanked hers and didn't even bother to look at the charm in her hand.

"Look, I got a ring," Alicia's best friend, Tamara said, gently holding her charm in her palm. "I'm the next to get engaged!"

"I got a four-leaf clover for luck!"

"Mine is a couple in love. I think it means that I'm the next to marry!"

The girls' excited squeals did nothing to improve Alexis's sour moor. Rolling her eyes, she walked over to where Claire and Morgan were waiting for her.

"Which one did you get?" Claire asked, laughing at her friend's lack of enthusiasm. She shrugged and tossed the charm to her.

Morgan looked on as Claire held the charm up to the light for a closer look. "Oh, my God!" they both exclaimed.

"What? What is it?" she asked, reacting to the horrified looks on their faces. "I told you I would get the grim reaper charm!" she said, snatching the ribbon from Claire. "Let me see."

Alexis held the tiny silver charm at eye level and what she saw made her feel light-headed and sick to her stomach. A small, silver baby carriage was tied to the ribbon.

"What the hell is this supposed to mean?" she asked, laughing nervously.

"It means that you'll be next to have a baby," Morgan said cautiously. "Bullshit!" she said, tossing the charm back at Claire as if it were red-hot. Instead of reaching out to catch it, Claire took a frantic step back, letting the ominous charm fall with a soft clang to the floor. Morgan gazed at it as if transfixed by its supposed power.

"I am not pregnant!" she insisted, shaking her head.

"Are you sure?" Morgan asked, quickly picking up the charm from the floor when Alicia walked past and gave the three of them the evil eye.

"Of course I'm sure. I haven't even had sex in the past month," she said, taking a seat and still shaking her head.

"It's just superstition. It's silly," Claire said, nonetheless refusing to hold the charm.

"Exactly. That's why I didn't want to do it in the first place."

"What didn't you want to do?" a deep and very familiar voice asked, coming up behind Alexis and causing her breath to catch in her throat. Her heart began to beat faster, her cheeks became warm and tingled with unexpected happiness.

"Hey, Massai, you made it!" Claire exclaimed, turning around in her seat and patting his hand.

"You knew he was coming?" Alexis asked in disbelief.

"Of course I knew. Who do you think told him where the reception was?"

Alexis was speechless. The last time they'd spoken, Massai had told her that he planned to take it easy this weekend. She was completely surprised.

"Are you going to give me a kiss, a hug, a handshake? Anything?" Massai asked, smiling down at her like the cat that swallowed the canary.

Words and movement failed her. She clearly remembered telling Massai that she didn't think it would be a good idea for him to visit Detroit until he had settled things with Eva and now there he was, standing in front of her in a tuxedo with a dimpled smile so bright it was blinding. He looked better than a knight in shining armor.

"What are you doing here?" she asked, finally finding her voice.

"Why? Do you have a date or something?" Massai asked looking around as if he expected her escort to come strolling in at any moment.

"No, I don't have a date, but I thought we had an understanding."

"We did, but all that was taken care of this morning. I'm here for four days, and I thought you would be happy."

Now it was time for Alexis to put up or shut up. When she told him what he needed to do, she never expected him to actually follow through with it. Making that deal with him was simply another ploy to protect her herself. While she knew in her heart that she was falling in love with him completely and totally, she was still apprehensive about taking their relationship to the next level. It was easy to keep her feelings and emotions at bay when Massai was in New Orleans, but now that he was in her hometown, in her space, and she looked at him, Alexis knew her fortitude was on its last leg.

"We'll just leave you two alone," Morgan said, as she and Claire made a quick getaway, but not before pressing the baby-carriage charm into Alexis's palm and winking.

"Aren't you happy?" Massai said, hurt and confusion written all over his face.

Alexis stood and smoothed the wrinkles out of her dress. "Of course I'm happy. I'm surprised, too."

"That was the whole point. I wanted to surprise you."

"Well, you definitely succeeded."

"Where's my kiss?" he asked, smiling again.

"Here? In front of everybody?" she asked, mortified.

"It's a wedding, Alexis, not a jail cell. I'm sure no one will mind."

Massai took her in his arms and kissed her lips softly. "How are you?" he whispered against her mouth, causing her to inhale his sweet, winter-fresh breath.

"I'm happy," Alexis realized and replied honestly.

19

SURPRISE

"So where are you going to go?" Carlos asked Eva as they lay in bed after an especially sweaty session of sex. "You can always move in here with me."

She sat up in bed and reached for her half-empty pack of cigarettes. Seeing Carlos wasn't the only thing she had to keep from Massai; her long time smoking habit was another. "I'm not going to have to leave. I have a plan," she said, lighting the cigarette and inhaling long and deep.

"Yeah, right. We both know how well your plans work," he said sarcastically.

"How was I supposed to know that he wouldn't want to have sex anymore?"

"From what you've been telling me, I don't think any plan you come up with will work. I think he's pretty much gone over to this new chick."

"This plan isn't new; it's just a variation on the one from before."

"Okay . . ."

"I'm going to just lie and say that I'm pregnant to buy myself some time. Granted, Massai probably won't be all that happy about the idea, but I know him, and there isn't any way that he'll abandon me if he thinks I'm carrying his baby."

"He's not going to believe you."

"He will believe me if I show him a positive pregnancy test. I can just get my friend Bridget to take one of those home things. She's six months already, so I'm sure her reading will be completely positive."

"Well, what are you going to do when you don't start showing in a few months?"

"I'll just fake a miscarriage. By then I will have redeemed myself as his girlfriend and we will both be in so much pain from the loss of our baby that there is no way he'll break up with me."

Carlos stared at her as she blew smoke rings into the air. "You're crazier than I thought," he said, shaking his head and wondering what kind of woman he had gotten himself involved with.

"I am not crazy. I'm ambitious and I know what I want. You act as though I said I was going to hold a gun to his head or something."

"No, but you are trying to trap him with some fake-ass baby. If you would do that to him, there is no telling what you are capable of doing to me."

"What do you propose I do, since you have so much to say?"

"Eva, you just need to face facts and let that man be. He is with somebody else. What about that is so hard for you to accept?" he asked, becoming frustrated, irritated and agitated all at once.

"The part where I come out of this broke and homeless. He owes me and I'm getting ready to collect."

"What does he owe you? I have never once seen you in a jersey running down a basketball court on ESPN."

"I don't have to actually play the game to be owed something. What about all those times I sat up in the stands bored to death? Or when I had his bath ready for him when he walked through the door?"

"That's part of being a good girlfriend; I expect the same thing, and I shouldn't have to pay you for it."

"I don't even like basketball. And I thought you were on my side?"

"I was until this plan started getting out of hand. I really don't understand why you just won't let this go. I make enough money to support you."

"I deserve to be more than supported, Carlos. I deserve the best that life has to offer, and I don't think that those things are something you can afford on a daily basis," Eva said, flicking her ashes into a water glass.

Carlos got out of bed and looked down at her in disbelief. When he first met her, he really thought she was sweet and honest with just a little bit of a wild streak underneath. He had come to realize recently that what he thought was a wild streak was actually her deceptive and cutthroat tendencies. She was dangerous, and he was beginning to feel the need to cut all ties with her before it was too late.

"I really don't like what you're getting ready to do, Eva," he said from the bathroom.

"Why not?" she answered loudly. "Your pockets will be benefiting from this, too. It's just going to take a little longer than I thought. And you didn't have anything to say when I poked those holes in his condoms, Mr. Righteous."

"You didn't give me the chance. You just went ahead and did whatever it was that you wanted to do without even talking to me."

Eva smacked her lips and rolled her eyes but said nothing. "Look, Carlos, this is the plan and I'm sticking to it. Now as the guys in the hood say, you can either roll with me, or get rolled over."

"Why do you keep looking at me like that?" Alexis asked, nervously unlocking the door to her apartment.

"Because you're beautiful," Massai said, switching his duffle bags from one shoulder to the other.

"I'm sure you've met plenty of beautiful women in your time," she said, pushing the door open and stepping inside the darkened space.

"I have, but no one like you." He dropped his bags to the floor and drew her close for a kiss.

She felt as if she was living in a wonderful fantasy created for someone else. This was too good to be true. She pulled back from his embrace and walked over to the wall to flip the light switch. Alexis didn't want things to get too carried away before she asked the question that was really on her mind. "Since you're in Detroit, I assume you and Eva are no longer together?"

"I thought we already went over that," he said, reaching for her again. But she stepped back and folded her arms across her chest.

"That vague answer you gave me at the wedding was not going over anything."

"Okay, I see that you aren't going to welcome me as a guest until we talk about this situation, so what is it that you want to know?"

"I want to know what you said to her."

"I threw her ass out, and that's all I'm going to say!" Massai responded, loudly recreating a scene from *Lean on Me*.

She laughed, immediately recognizing the quote. "Okay, Joe Clark, I'm serious."

"I told her that I met someone, that I was in love and I expected her to be gone when I got back."

She didn't know how to respond. She wasn't sure if her mind was playing tricks on her, but she could have sworn he had just admitted to being in love with her.

"Did you hear me? I said that I'm in love with you," he repeated.

"Massai, are you sure?" she whispered. Alexis felt the same way, but didn't know if she was ready to tell him.

"Of course I'm sure, and if you don't feel the same way yet, that's cool. I know what an ice queen you can be," he joked.

"I am not an ice queen. I'm cautious."

"Whatever you say, Alexis." Loosening his tie, he asked, "Are you going to give me a tour of your place or what?"

Holding hands, they took the short tour of her apartment and ended up, finally, in her bedroom.

"This is where I sleep." She walked over to the bedside table and turned on the lamp, dimly lighting the room.

"And where will I be sleeping tonight?" Massai asked, lifting her hand to his mouth and kissing it softly.

"You can stay wherever you feel most comfortable, the guest bedroom or the couch . . . my bedroom . . ."

"It's not about where I feel comfortable, but where you're comfortable having me."

Alexis thought back to their last night in New Orleans. She remembered going into Malik's guesthouse determined not to let things go any further than kissing, hugging and cuddling. But as soon as he had touched her, all self-control went out the window. She knew it would be pointless to put up a front, to pretend she really didn't want to be with him when she did. How could she deny it when making love to him filled her thoughts day and night?

"Massai," she said, taking a deep breath, "I want you with me in my bed."

He smiled at her, showing his dimples, "Then that's exactly where I want to be."

20

MIDNIGHT LOVE

"Turn around," Massai gently commanded Alexis.

Trembling slightly, she turned around, her back to him. He reached down and slowly unzipped the back of her dress.

"Are you sure you want to do this?" he asked, bending down to kiss her bare shoulder.

"I was sure in New Orleans."

She let her dress fall to the floor, kicking it across the room, the blue silk landing on the floor near the closet door. Alexis stood before Massai in nothing but a white thong, matching strapless bra and lace-trimmed thigh-highs.

Massai turned her around and took in her form from head to toe. He took off his jacket and tossed it across the room; it came to rest in a heap atop her dress. "Damn, you are perfect," he marveled, simultaneously kissing her and walking her over to the bed. Placing his hand at the small of her back, he gently guided her body down onto the soft bedding, never taking his mouth off hers.

Alexis's heart was pounding furiously and while she was excited, her nervousness nearly overshadowed her arousal. She was amazed; she hadn't been this anxious about being intimate with a man since she lost her virginity.

She unbuttoned Massai's shirt and slipped it off. His muscles rippled as he balanced himself over her while running his hands down the length of her body.

"You don't have to be scared," he said, sensing her apprehension. "I'll only do what you want me to." He removed her thigh-highs and kissed her from her ankles to her navel.

He slowly removed her remaining garments, paying strict attention to every part of her body. He spent the next hour massaging, caressing, kissing and worshipping her figure.

Finally, Massai reached into his tuxedo pants pocket and retrieved three condoms. He and stripped down to his black boxer shorts; holding the condom in his left hand. As their kisses deepened and became more passionate, Alexis removed Massai's boxers and hesitantly held his erection in her hands. He placed the condom in her hand, and she unrolled the latex onto his smooth skin.

He entered her deeply, causing her to moan with pleasure. Her body movements mirrored his as they fell into an erotic slow dance of emotion and passion. He kissed her mouth, neck, shoulders and breasts, all the while moving smoothly between her legs.

"Massai . . ." Alexis whispered, placing her hands on his back to let him know she wanted and needed more. Their fingers intertwined, and she did not know where her body ended and his began. "Massai . . ." she called out again, feeling a level of desire she never knew existed.

"I love you," he whispered in her ear, slowing his stroke.

"Massai . . ."

"I love you, Alexis," he repeated, moving through her body, heart, mind and soul. "I love you," he said again, searching for a response in her tear-filled eyes.

"Don't hurt me, Massai," she said, the tears falling onto her pillow. Alexis wasn't speaking of the physical pain that sometimes accompanied sex but of the emotional pain that always came when she gave her heart away.

"I love you," he said once more, kissing the tears from her face.

She could fight no longer. Her feelings for Massai were much too strong. As scared as she was, she knew that she had to let go of the past and live in the present.

"I love you, too, Massai," she said, closing her eyes and saying a silent prayer that she hadn't just made the biggest mistake of her life.

21

THE MORNING AFTER

"Good morning," Massai said when Alexis's eyes blinked open. At first she thought she was dreaming, but when she felt Massai's lips on her own she knew that she wasn't.

"What time is it?" she asked pulling the white bed-sheet up around her chest while she used the other hand to push her hair back from her face.

"One-thirty."

"One-thirty! Why didn't you wake me up?" she asked, glancing at the digital clock.

"I didn't wake you up because you were obviously tired. I figured you would get up on your own when you were ready."

"How long have you been up?"

"Since eight. I ran around your apartment complex, took a shower, made breakfast and watched Sports-Center."

"Massai, you should have gotten me out of this bed. I would have loved to have gone running with you. " Alexis sat up and dangled her legs off the bed, her toes touching the carpet.

"You couldn't keep up," he laughed.

"I would have tried. I want to spend all the time with you that I possibly can, considering you're leaving in two days."

"Come with me."

"You know I start work in two weeks."

"Excuses, excuses. Why don't you come on out here and get some of this breakfast I made for you."

"Just give me a second to throw something on."

"Why can't you just come to breakfast like that?" Massai asked, tugging at the sheet she had wrapped around her body.

"That's gross, Massai," she said, looking at him skeptically but laughing at the idea.

"For who? I would love to look at you while I eat."

"There is no way I'm going to eat butt naked."

"Fine, just put this on and meet me in the kitchen." He tossed one of his cutoff shirts to her and left the bedroom. Walking past the heap of discarded formalwear into the bathroom, Alexis slipped the shirt over her head and looked at herself in the mirror.

A shirt that would normally fit Massai perfectly swallowed her and reached all the way down to her knees. Across the chest, big, bold block letters read 'New Orleans Hornets Basketball'. She brushed her teeth and washed her face and saw that she was glowing. She couldn't remember a time when she looked or felt this happy; she could become used to this feeling very quickly.

"What in the world are you doing in there?" he called.

"I'm coming, I'm coming." Alexis left the bathroom, and went into the main living area. Something smelled delicious. She joined him at the table and was shocked by the spread before her: Belgian waffles, whipped cream and strawberries. Two champagne flutes filled with Moet mimosa were at the head of each place setting.

"Am I supposed to believe that you did all this?" she asked as Massai pulled her chair out for her.

"Who else could have done it?"

"You didn't order anything and have it delivered?"

"Look at all the dirty dishes in the sink," he said, pointing to the soiled pots, pans and utensils overflowing the sink and spilling onto the counter.

Alexis rose slightly and looked. "And who's going to clean all that up?"

"Well, when I was growing up one person cooked and the other person did the dishes."

"I guess that's fair," she said grudgingly. She hated doing dishes and, even though she had a fully functioning dishwasher, just the thought of having to scrape and rinse all those dishes made her tired.

"Your phone rang early this morning after I got out of the shower."

"Did you answer it?"

"What if I did?" he asked, testing the waters, trying to see if she had anyone else waiting in the wings.

"Then I hope you took a message," she said, smiling at him and putting a piece of waffle into her mouth.

"I didn't answer; just let it ring."

"It was probably my mother. I'm sure she was shitting bricks after we left the wedding so quickly."

"You didn't introduce me to anybody. I'm starting to think that you're embarrassed by me," Massai said, piling a huge portion of strawberries onto his plate.

"You know I'm not embarrassed by you. It's just that yesterday I really didn't know *how* to introduce you. Actually, I still don't."

"I'm your man, Alexis, your significant other, your better half."

"Just like that, huh?" she asked, smiling across the table at him.

"Just like that."

The telephone rang, interrupting their intimate breakfast. "Hello?" she answered.

"Do you know what time it is? You were supposed to be over here at noon to help me with this potato salad!" her mother blared. Most of the time Dana was calm and soft-spoken, but if you made her angry there was no telling what would come out of her mouth.

"I forgot. I'm sorry," Alexis apologized, as Massai rinsed her empty plate and began loading the dishwasher.

"You sure are, especially for the way you left your sister's reception two hours early. Your brother told me that you got into a truck with some man."

"I was tired and ready to go."

"Everything is not always about you, Alexis, and I know whoever it was you left with is still over there. I can hear the sex in your voice."

"What? Mama, are you serious?" she asked, going over to help Massai with the dishes.

"As a heart attack. So are you going to bring him with you or what? Everyone is waiting to meet him," Dana said without taking a breath.

"Do I have a choice?" she asked, although she already knew the answer to that particular question.

"Not unless you want us all to come over there and barbeque in your bedroom. Now get your tail over here and bring whoever that is with you." With that, Alexis's mother hung up the phone.

Pressing the end button on the telephone, she took a deep breath. "Massai, we have to go to my parents' house for a little get-together. Now if you don't want to go, I completely understand, but I really don't have a choice in the matter."

"Of course I want to go. Do you think I would pass up a chance to meet the people who created you?"

She rolled her eyes and laughed. "Well, we'd better get going. I was supposed to be over there two hours ago."

"So I guess that means that a quickie is out of the question?" he said, stepping in front of her and lifting her shirt above her hips.

"That depends on how quick of a quickie you're talking about."

Massai grabbed her firmly around the waist and lifted her up onto the counter. "Not that quick."

Two and a half hours and one bubble bath later, Alexis and Massai were finally en route to her parents' home.

"Are you nervous?" she asked, exiting the Southfield Freeway.

"No. Should I be?" he asked, trying to maneuver his legs comfortably in the passenger's seat of Alexis's Scion TC.

"I would be if I were you, especially considering how important it is to my parents that all their children get married. I'm the last one."

"I doubt that they will be thinking about marrying you off so soon after Alicia's wedding."

"You would be surprised."

She turned down her parents' tree-lined street and felt her stomach completing three somersaults as she pulled into the very end of the circular driveway. Cars were jammed down the narrow street, making her more nervous at the prospect of having to introduce Massai to more than just immediate family members.

"Are you ready?" he asked excitedly, setting both feet on the pavement.

She cut the car's engine, removed the key from the ignition and reluctantly closed the car door behind her.

Her brother, Aaron, opened the front door to the house and jogged down the porch stairs. The family's golden retriever, King, bounded down the stars behind him, nearly mowing down Alexis in the process.

"I know you," he said, bending down to attach the red leash around King's neck. He straightened and shook

Massai's hand. "You play for New Orleans, don't you? Massai Taylor, right?"

"And you must be Aaron? Nice to meet you, man," he said.

"You know we could really use someone like you on the Pistons right now. What do you average? About fifteen, twenty points a game?" Aaron asked, as if he worked for Joe Dumars.

"Something like that," Massai proudly confirmed.

"Wait until my dad meets you."

"Excuse me? Is he the only person you see standing here?" Alexis asked playfully.

"I see you all the time," her brother said, ruffling her hair with his leash-free hand. "Everybody's waiting for you in the back, and let me warn you now: Mama is not happy."

"Let's just go back to my place," she suggested, tugging at Massai's arm as he started in the direction of the backyard.

"No, Alexis. I think you're making it out to be worse than it is." He held her hand tightly as they walked toward the sound of the music and the smell of the food.

"It's about time you got your tail over here," Alexis's mother said, meeting them at the gate. Hugging her daughter, she continued talking. "With Alicia gone on her honeymoon and you doing God only knows what, I had to prepare all this food by myself—as usual." Dana turned her head up, using her hand to shield her eyes from the sun. "So you're the reason my child couldn't get over here to help me?"

"Mama!" Alexis said, mortified.

"What's your name and what do you do?" she asked, ignoring her daughter and directing her question to Massai.

"My name is Massai Taylor. I play professional basketball, and it is a pleasure to meet you, Mrs. Hunter."

"It's nice to finally meet you, too, sweetie. I've heard about you, though I'm sorry to say that I don't know very much."

"Well, I hope we have a chance to fix that," he said, laying on the charm.

"So how long have you two been seeing each other?" her mother asked, getting back to business.

"Mama!" Alexis interjected again.

"About a month and a half," he smilingly answered.

"Is this serious or just a stopover, because her father and I won't stand for you getting your milk for free."

"Mama, stop!" Alexis said, stamping her foot in the grass.

"I'm very serious about your daughter, Mrs. Hunter," he said, squeezing her hand reassuringly.

"Call me Dana. Since you say you're so serious, I assume that you have plans to ask her to marry you in the near future?" she asked sweetly.

"Look, that is enough!" Alexis said angrily, by now completely beside herself. "We have known each other less than two months, and Massai, you do not have to answer that question."

"I don't mind answering."

"Well, I mind. This is ridiculous, Mama. We came here to have a good time, not to be interrogated!"

Dana threw up her hands in surrender. "Fine, fine, I'm sorry. But I don't know how you can blame me, considering you never tell me anything."

Alexis was fuming and at that particular moment, had nothing more to say to her mother. "I'm going to go get something to eat," she said, stalking off across the lawn toward the food-laden table.

"Mrs. Hunter, Dana, it was really nice to meet you."

"Nice meeting you, too, Massai. I had almost given up on Alexis as far as marriage was concerned. You know she's been hurt several times?"

"I'm aware of that, and I don't plan on adding to that list," he said earnestly.

"I hope not," Dana said, patting his arm gently. "I don't think my baby's heart can take another blow."

22

PLATINUM AND DIAMONDS

"Where are you?" Malik yelled into the phone, sounding more like Massai's father than his best friend. "Do you know I damn near called the police to have them issue an Amber Alert for your ass?"

"You can't call in an Amber Alert for a grown man," he said, walking through Somerset Collection shopping mall.

"Missing persons, then. You know what I'm talking about. I called your house, your cell and your mama's, and nobody knew where you were."

"You called my mama's?"

"Hell, yeah! I thought someone had kidnapped you. So are you going to tell me where you are or not?"

"I'm at the mall."

"Can I get a city, please?"

"Troy."

"Troy, what? Where is Troy?"

"The mall is in Troy, Michigan. It's a suburb outside of Detroit, super sleuth."

"Oh, so you're with Alexis?"

"Damn, you have a lot of questions," Massai said, entering the store he had been searching for.

"I'm just asking."

"Yes, I did come to Detroit to visit Alexis, but right now she's at her yoga class."

"So what the hell are you doing at the mall if you're not with her? How did you find the mall if you're not with her?"

"Is this twenty questions or what? I'm at the mall to shop. What do you think I'm here for? And have you ever heard of the Internet? MapQuest?"

"What are you going to buy?"

"Why are you asking me so many questions? You need something to do so that you can stay out of my business."

"Massai, you called me."

"Only after you blew up my cellphone like some woman."

"What store are you in?"

"Footlocker."

"Couldn't you have come up with a better lie than that? Why would you be in Footlocker when we get gym shoes for free? Now what store are you in?"

"Cartier," he said, finally coming clean.

"What are you buying in Cartier? And I really hope it's a pair of cufflinks."

"Not quite," Massai said, switching his cellphone from one ear to the other.

"I think I know what it is, but I'm praying that I'm wrong."

"Then I won't tell you; I would hate for you to be disappointed."

"No, tell me."

"I'm getting Alexis a ring," he said, signaling a sales representative.

"I hope it's a friendship ring," Malik said, but suspecting he was probably way off base.

"Engagement ring," he answered, not allowing the misgivings he heard in his friend's voice to deter him.

"I'm going to fly up there and bring you back to New Orleans before you go and do something crazy."

"I don't think that will be necessary."

"Do you hear yourself? You are getting ready to ask this girl to marry you and you've barely known her two months!"

"What's your point?" Massai asked, informing the Cartier representative that he was ready for his appointment.

"My point is that you are not thinking this through. Last time we talked, you told me that you were getting ready to put Eva out, and now you're in Detroit buying an engagement ring for some other chick. You are not making any sense. You don't even know her."

"I know enough. Yesterday we came back to her place after visiting her family, and I just sat and watched her for like an hour. She was walking around in an old pair of pajamas, and I literally couldn't take my eyes off her. She is completely amazing and there is no way that I will be satisfied with just a long-distance relationship."

"Spare me the sickening details," Malik said dryly. "If she's all that you say she is, then why not bring her down to New Orleans and move her in with you? Why do you have to jump the broom?"

"That's not good enough for her. I can shack up with anybody, but I want to be with this woman for the rest of my life."

"You are completely gone. I mean, Tom Cruise over Katie Holmes gone. If I didn't know better I would say you're on something. Another one bites the dust," Malik said regretfully.

"I've never been a player," Massai said, sitting down in the chocolate-brown leather chair and examining the five diamond rings the saleswoman had placed in front of him.

"I know, but I've always had hope for you. Have you at least gotten a little closer to the panties, or are you waiting for the honeymoon?" Malik laughed.

"You know I handle mine."

"That's what I'm afraid of."

From the moment the couple entered Seldom Blues, Massai's heart wouldn't stop racing and his palms were clammy. As the host led them to their table, he felt about twenty sets of eyes boring into his back. Loud whispers assaulted his ears: "Doesn't he play basketball? What is his name?" As a professional athlete, he was used to this kind of thing when he went out in public, but tonight it made him especially nervous. All of these people would be the first to know whether or not there would be a wedding in his future.

Massai and Alexis had gotten through drinks, appetizers, salad and the main course without a hitch, but if he was going to propose, it would have to be soon because she declined dessert, opting for a glass of wine.

He waited for Alexis to return from the restroom, holding the ring in his hand. This was the fifth time that evening he'd gone into his pocket to look at the four-carat, platinum canary diamond. The ring, as unique as the woman he loved, sparkled in the dim light of the jazz club.

"They have a really nice bathroom," Alexis said, sliding back into her seat before he could stand and pull it out for her.

He closed his fist tightly around the ring box and shoved it back into his blazer pocket.

"Are you okay, Massai? You've been acting really weird all night," she asked with concern.

"I'm okay."

"Are you sure? I think you're catching a cold or something. You're all quiet, and why are you sweating like that?"

"I'm okay, baby; it's just hot in here," he said, wiping his brow with a linen napkin and trying to assure her that everything was normal. She was looking toward the bar and bobbing her head to the live band when he noticed a change in her expression. She went from looking happy to looking as if she had just seen a ghost.

"Oh, shit," she said, wanting to shrink and disappear as a very familiar face strode confidently toward their table.

"Well, well, well. What do we have here?" Kevin said, stopping at Alexis's side and smiling down at her as if he had just won the lottery.

"Hello, Kevin," she said, keeping her voice steady even though it was her turn to sweat bullets. Massai raised his eyebrows but remained silent.

"I wanted to call you to let you know that I had a wonderful time at brunch, we should really do it again sometime," Kevin said, looking straight at Massai with a smirk. "Aren't you going to introduce me to your friend?"

"Um, of course. Kevin, this is Massai. Massai, this is Kevin," Alexis said. Her nervousness and her unease were beginning to show. Instead of shaking hands, the two men just glared at each other silently. She felt the tension in the air and knew that if she didn't get rid of Kevin quickly, the entire scene could become very ugly.

23

GET UP! GET OUT!

"Mind if I pull up a chair?" Kevin asked, breaking the silence that descended over the table.

"Yes, I mind. We're having dinner, Kevin," Alexis said angrily.

"What about you, Massai?"

Massai shifted in his seat uncomfortably, and the scowl never left his face. "Please be my guest," he said, using his long arm to yank the chair away from the table.

"Don't you two make a cute couple? Look more like brother and sister than boyfriend and girlfriend. Kind of incestuous, if you ask me."

"Nobody asked you," Massai said, glowering.

"What do you want, Kevin?" she asked.

"Just to get to know my replacement man to man."

"Where is your wife tonight? At home with the kids?" Massai asked pointedly, recognizing Kevin as the married man who had played Alexis like a fiddle before they met.

"Ex-wife. We're in the process of divorce."

"This is unbelievable," she cut in.

"Did you know, Massai, that if I hadn't been married, Alexis and I would still be together?"

"I seriously doubt that." Massai felt his chest rise and fall. Under the crisp white tablecloth, his fists opened and closed as if preparing for battle.

"Kevin, I think it's time for you to go," she said, touching Massai's leg under the table and feeling it contract with anger.

"Just one more thing before I go," Kevin said, looking directly at Massai with a smirk. "I just want to make sure that you understand that you're the rebound guy. She is only with you because she can't have me." Kevin rose from the table and looked at Alexis before causally running his index finger down her bare arm.

"So you're just going to disrespect me and my girl?" Massai said angrily, rising from the table. He walked towards him and stared down, feeling the urge to beat Kevin's brains out.

"What are you going to do? Hit me? Go ahead. I know who you are, and I'll take a beat-down for all the money I'll get in court for my pain and suffering. I can see the news crawl right now . . . MASSAI TAYLOR, OF THE NEW ORLEANS HORNETS, JAILED IN DETROIT FOR ASSAULT AND BATTERY," Kevin laughed, his posture daring Massai to take another step.

Massai's nostrils flared and his jaws tightened. Deathly afraid he would hit Kevin, Alexis jumped up and stood between the two men. Laughing, Kevin walked back to the table where his date was waiting.

"Let's go," Massai said furiously, throwing three one hundred-dollar bills on the table, clearly overpaying for dinner.

"I'm sorry."

"Let's go," he said again, his voice low and firm. He began taking long strides toward the exit, and she had to jog slightly to keep up with him.

The car was waiting at the curb, and instead of opening the door for her as he normally did, he walked over to the driver's seat, climbed in and slammed the door. He barely waited for Alexis to get inside before he tore off from the restaurant, leaving the odor of burned tires behind them.

"Massai, let's talk about this," she begged.

"What's there to talk about? That nigga said everything he wanted to say, touched you, and there was nothing you did to stop him."

"I asked him to leave, Massai. What else could I do?"

"How about confirming the fact that I'm your man? Or, how about denying that you're with me because you can't be with him? And what was that shit about the two of you having brunch together?"

"We met for brunch because he said he wanted to apologize for the way he had treated me. As soon as he started talking all that get-back-together stuff, I left. And I didn't think I needed to give you confirmation. I'm with you because I love you and you make me happy."

"Well, why didn't you tell him that?"

"Because I don't have to. The way we feel about each other has nothing to do with him. He only said all those things because he's jealous and wanted to get a rise out of you."

"Do you still have feelings for him or something?"

"What are you talking about?" Alexis asked, becoming frustrated.

"You didn't seem to mind too much when he was feeling all on you."

"Massai, he was not feeling on me. He touched my arm, and if I had said something, it would have just made the situation worse."

"I don't think it could have gotten any worse. The entire night is ruined," he said, more to himself than to her.

They drove the rest of the way to her apartment in tense silence. He parked the car, got out and walked up to the door, all before she could put her high-heels down on the pavement.

After unlocking the front door and entering the apartment, she tried to put the incident behind them and enjoy what was left of the evening. "Why don't we take a bath to—" Alexis began. Massai slammed the door to the guest bedroom and locked it behind him.

She stared at the white-wood door in despair. She honestly could not understand Massai's reaction. Granted, the episode with Kevin at the restaurant was unpleasant, but this was their last night together and she wanted it to be special.

She knocked softly on the door three times. "Massai, can I come in?"

No answer.

"Massai . . ."

Still no answer.

"You know what? You're acting completely ridiculous!" Alexis herself was becoming angry. "I can't believe you're trying to put the blame on me when you are the one who invited him to sit down! When you pulled out the chair for him, did you think he would be cordial? He's jealous of you, Massai. He wants me and can't have me, so he's jealous. Don't you get it? This is what he wanted to happen," she yelled through the door.

He heard every word but refused to answer. He knew he was acting childish, but wasn't ready to face her. He sat on the bed holding the canary diamond between his fingers. On the ride back from the restaurant, he had seriously contemplated packing his bags and catching the next plane back to New Orleans. Never in his life had something like that happened to him, and as angry as he was, he knew that Kevin had been right. If he put one finger on him, he would have called the police immediately and would have filed a civil suit for millions of dollars.

He listened to Alexis's footsteps fade and heard the door to her bedroom slam shut with a force that rocked the entire apartment. Massai heard the pipes rattle as she turned on the shower and let the water run. His heart softened and ached as he thought about the tears that she would wash away in the shower. As angry as he still was, he began to accept that Alexis was right. His anger was misdirected, and he had fallen right into the trap that Kevin set for him.

Steeling himself, Massai went to Alexis's room and stepped inside. He could hear the sounds of her soaping up and rinsing off. He took a deep breath before pushing the bathroom door open and smelling her milk-and-honey body-wash.

"Alexis, I need to talk to you."

"I'm busy," she said, her voice tight with attitude and anger, reminding him of the unapproachable woman he had met two months ago at The House of Blues.

"It'll just take a minute."

"What? Are you leaving? I'm not getting out to show you to the door. You know where it is. It was nice while it lasted," Alexis said, thanking God that he couldn't see the tears her voice didn't betray.

"I'm not leaving."

"Well then, whatever it is can wait, can't it?"

"No, it's important," he said, holding the ring in his hand.

"Important to whom? The only thing that's important to me right now is taking this shower and going to bed, and that's exactly what I intend to do."

"So you won't get out?" he asked, taking off his shoes, socks and blazer.

"No," Alexis answered stubbornly.

Massai yanked back the shower curtain and stepped inside, still in his jeans and striped shirt.

"Are you crazy? You still have on all your clothes!" she said, stepping back to make space for Massai in the tiny shower.

"I said I needed to talk to you. You wouldn't come out, so I really didn't have a choice," he said, feeling the water soak through his clothes, making his jeans feel like weights attached to his legs.

"Whatever it is, I'm sure it could have waited fifteen minutes."

Massai took her left hand from her hips and quickly slipped the ring on her wet finger before he lost the nerve. "This couldn't wait."

Alexis looked down at the most beautiful ring she had ever seen. The heavy platinum ring held so many canary-yellow diamonds that it was impossible to count them all.

"What is this for?" she asked, staring down at the huge ring on her left hand.

"This is what I wanted to give you at dinner."

"What is it for, Massai? What does it mean?"

By now his clothes were completely soaked, but he plunged ahead, seemingly unfazed. "Since I have been here with you, I have come to realize more than ever that you are the one I want to spend the rest of my life with. I need to see you up in the stands during games; I want to rub your back when you're pregnant with my babies. You are it for me. You are my beginning and my end. Alexis, you are the one I've been waiting for my entire life, and I want you to be my wife."

Alexis had dreamed of this moment since she was a little girl. The man she loved had asked her to marry him. Never had she envisioned it would happen standing in a shower with a fully dressed man. But none of that mattered now. She was in love, and when she closed her eyes and saw her future, there were no moments when Massai was not at her side.

"I can't believe this is happening," she whispered, looking up at him and back down at the ring.

"I want you to follow your heart."

"My heart belongs to you, Massai. It has from the moment we met in New Orleans."

"I need an answer," he said, smiling down at her, already knowing her response.

"Of course I'll marry you." She had barely gotten it out before he took her into his arms and kissed her, emotion and happiness pouring from his lips.

"Let's get out of this shower," he said, attempting to turn off the water.

"No, stay," she said, grasping his arm. She took off his wet clothes and placed hungry kisses on his chest and stomach.

Massai's large hands cupped her bottom and, in one seamless motion, lifted her up against the wet tile and entered her without hesitation. Alexis wrapped her bronzed legs around his waist and took in every inch of him. It was amazing how her body seemed to be tailor-made for him. Never in her life had a man made her feel all these different things at once: love, lust, passion—all meshing and causing her body to tremble and call out for more.

He responded to her requests, giving her exactly what she wanted. He moved so deeply inside her she thought her spine would shatter.

They stayed that way until the water turned cold and their skin wrinkled. Not wanting to stop, he carried her to her bedroom and gently placed her down on the carpet. They continued their explorations of each other until dawn.

24

KEEP YOUR FRIENDS CLOSE

"So now that Massai's gone maybe you'll call us some-time?" Claire said to Alexis. The three friends sat at Beans and Cornbread waiting for the waitress to bring the lunch platters.

"I'm sorry, but I barely came up for air," she explained, tearing a sugar packet open and shaking it into her iced tea.

"It was that good, huh?" Morgan asked.

"None of your business; I do not kiss and tell."

"So what are your plans? Will the two of you con-tinue to see each other or what?" Claire asked.

"Well, that's why I wanted you to meet me here." Alexis dug into her purse and slid on the canary diamond engagement ring under the table. "I'm getting married!" she announced, happily flashing the ring at her friends.

The excited reaction she expected from Claire and Morgan was missing, and instead, silence fell over the table.

"Did you hear me? I said that I'm getting married! Massai asked me last night after we had dinner at Seldom Blues, which turned out horrible, but that's a whole other story."

Claire and Morgan were still silent but kept staring at her as if she had one eye.

"Aren't you happy for me? We can start planning the wedding right away. Massai said that money is no object and the sooner the better."

"Alexis, slow down," Claire said, looking at her with concern.

"You mean to tell me that some random guy you met two months ago proposed to you, and I've been with Craig a million years, and I can't even get a Valentine's Day card out of him? Something is very wrong with this picture," Morgan said, peevishly throwing her napkin onto the table.

The smile that was hanging onto Alexis's face by a thread faded away altogether. "Oh, I get it," she said, looking at her friends from across the table. "It's cool when you're the only one in a committed relationship, Morgan. And Claire, you can only handle being supportive when we're both alone."

"You are jumping to conclusions, Alexis. I'm just concerned that this thing with Massai is starting to move way too fast. I want you to be happy, but I also want you to be smart," Claire said, putting her hand over Alexis's. She snatched it away, her eyes flashing.

"I never would have thought you two would pull this on me," she said, shaking her head.

"Pull what? Being concerned and questioning things that are of concern is what any good friend would do. If I sat here and let you marry this guy without so much as saying 'boo', then what kind of friend would I be?"

"Okay, I'm sorry. I am a little bit jealous, but I think I have a right to be," Morgan said, pouting like a two year old.

"You don't have a right to be. Maybe if you and your man didn't go around cheating on each other you wouldn't be in this position," Alexis shot back.

"What are you talking about?"

"Everyone knows that Craig is a hoe, and please don't forget about your little pool-table incident back down in New Orleans," she reminded Morgan, bringing her back to reality and closing her mouth for the time being.

"All I'm saying is this . . . did you really think all of this through, or are you just jumping the gun?" Claire asked after she regained Alexis's attention.

"Of course I thought it through. I love him, he loves me and that is all that matters."

"Where will you live? Will you work or be a housewife? How many kids will the two of you have? Have you even met his parents?" Claire shot questions at her like an automatic weapon.

"All of those decisions will be made in due time," she answered, slightly embarrassed that she didn't know the answers and couldn't say that she had met his parents.

"I think now is the perfect time, because if you wait until you get married and his answers don't match yours, then what? Somebody is going to have to compromise for the sake of the relationship or there will be no relationship."

"Well, obviously we'll have to live in New Orleans because of his job, unless he gets traded somewhere else."

"So you're basically saying that you will follow him anywhere?" Morgan butted in, emerging from her funk.

"Yes, I will," Alexis confirmed.

"Good, now we're getting somewhere. Will you work?" Claire continued as the waiter placed their lunches in front of them.

"Yes, I'll work. I didn't go to college all those years to sit up in the house and wait for my man to get home."

"And you'll be doing a lot of waiting, considering he'll be on the road for about forty-one games a year."

"People sacrifice for love," she said, smiling.

"You sound like a Hallmark card."

"Wait a minute. I'm confused as to why all of a sudden you have fifty questions when you are the one who kept insisting that Massai and I get together?"

"I think you are misunderstanding me. Morgan and I like Massai and want you to be happy," Claire said, looking to a nodding Morgan for support. "But the fact is that both of you have just gotten out of relationships. I think it would be a better idea if the two of you moved in together."

"What? I think you two are the ones who are misunderstanding some things. I did not come here to get your approval or ask permission to get married. I came here to share my news with friends. I need help planning my wedding, not my life. It would mean a lot to me if my two best friends would help me, but if you can't or won't then fine; I'll handle everything myself. Your invitations will be in the mail," Alexis said, getting up from the table and leaving her untouched food and unsupportive friends behind.

Anger bubbled to the surface when Massai pulled into his driveway and saw Eva's Lexus sitting outside as if it still belonged there. He was not naïve enough to believe that she would leave the car on the way to her new life, so he knew she would be waiting for him when his size sixteens stepped into the foyer. Not bothering to park his car in the garage, he jumped out and hurried to the front door.

The entire plane ride back to New Orleans had been filled with thoughts of the future he and Alexis would share. Several times he found himself wanting to stand in the aisle and announce to his fellow passengers that he was in love. Now, however, an uneasy feeling cast a shadow over the joy he had been feeling from the moment she had agreed to marry him. His stomach felt queasy when he thought about all the drama he was going to have to endure in a matter of seconds.

"It's about time you got back!" Eva greeted him just as he had anticipated.

"Didn't I tell you that I wanted you gone when I got back into town?"

"We need to talk. I didn't call you because I wanted to give you time to play house and get whatever it was out of your system."

"You know what? This is my fault; I should have had a locksmith come over here and change the locks."

"Massai, this is serious," Eva said, getting her purse from the table in the middle of the entryway.

"You think everything is serious that pertains to you. What happened this time? Did you break a nail?"

"No, smart ass, I'm pregnant."

He looked at her and saw her mouth moving, but his mind could not process what she was saying.

"What did you say?" he asked, shaking his head in an effort to clear it.

"I said I'm pregnant."

A nervous laughed escaped his lips. "You're playing, right?" His comment was more of a prayer than a question.

"I wish I was playing, because if there is one thing I hate to do, it is wearing out my welcome."

He thought back to the day he had left and instructed her to leave. She hadn't been very concerned about wearing out her welcome then. "You're lying, Eva."

"I'm not, Massai. I found out while you were on your little excursion. I figured things would work out much better if I waited until you got back to tell you."

"I don't believe you, Eva," he said, shaking his head.

"Well, you really don't have a choice, do you?" she said, beginning to show her true colors.

"Yeah, I have a choice. Am I supposed to just take you at your word when you have a history of telling bald-faced lies to me without so much as a flinch? I know what you're trying to do, and it is not going to work."

"And exactly what is it that you think I'm trying to do?"

"Trap me. I see it happen all the time."

"Massai, please. You are reading way too much into this. Why would I need to trap you when I can basically have any man I want? But since you want to play the conspiracy-theory role, let me show you my proof."

Eva dug into her purse and pulled out two items.

"These are both positive pregnancy tests; one from home and one from my doctor's office," she said, holding out the items with a satisfied smirk on her face. "Do you believe me now?"

25

SEX, LIES AND DEFEAT

Massai ignored the home-pregnancy test stick and snatched the piece of paper from Eva's hand. He searched it frantically, trying to find anything suspicious, but came up empty. Doctor's professional letterhead, chicken-scratch signature and medical jargon confirming Eva's claims were all there.

"Satisfied?" she asked, placing the stick back inside her purse.

Massai angrily threw the paper to the floor. "It's not mine. We both know you're a hoe. Hell, the whole city of New Orleans knows that. I would be surprised if you could narrow the father down to three," he spat, looking at her in disgust. The more he thought about it, the more he wished he had taken Malik's advice and gotten rid of her a long time ago.

"Is that any way to talk to the mother of your child?"

"It's not mine," Massai repeated slowly and deliberately.

"It is, Massai. The doctor says that I'm about eight weeks, and I haven't slept with anyone else."

"It's not mine."

"Oh, I see. Now you're going to pull the 'I'm a NBA superstar' bullshit on me. Denying your child, Massai? I thought you were better than that. I did not make this baby alone, and I will not take care of it alone. You've got the proof right here. Now are you going to be a man or a coward?"

Even though something inside him screamed caution, the man inside him, the man his parents raised him to be, would not allow a child that could be his to be without its father.

Defeated, he walked over to the stairway and sat down, breathing loudly. "How could this happen?"

"It's called sex, Massai. Didn't your father ever talk to you about the birds and the bees?"

"You know that's not what I'm talking about. We used condoms, Eva. I have never once made a mistake or forgotten the condom. Not once!"

"Why do you sound so depressed? It's a baby, Massai. You've always wanted children," she said, coming to sit next to him on the stairs.

"Not like this."

"We can get married, Massai. Be a real family, a stable family."

Massai looked at Eva as if she had just grown two heads.

"There is no way we're getting married. I thought I made it clear four days ago that we are over."

"Don't say that, Massai. Don't you want your child growing up in an environment where the parents are in love with each other?"

"You can't make me love you, Eva."

"You still love me or you wouldn't be sitting here right now."

"I asked her to marry me, Eva. The woman I've been seeing is probably at home planning our wedding right now."

"What? You asked her to marry you? I've been here with you for over a year, and what have you asked me to do besides have sex?"

"You are not what I was looking for long-term. I thought so in the beginning, but you changed somewhere along the way."

"Are you serious? Then why have I been sticking around for so long?"

"Are you asking me or yourself? As far as I know, you are in it for the money and nothing else. I have tried to work out our problems time and time again, but you always have something more important to do. You stay out all night, sleep around on me and spend all my money. Eva, you are not the kind of woman I want to grow old with."

"And she is? Someone you met a few months ago?"

"Look, I don't have to explain myself or my decisions to you. Alexis and I are getting married."

"So where does that leave me? Where does that leave our baby?"

"Child support and joint custody."

"That's not what you want for your child and you know it. Why don't we just talk about this and try to work it out? We can come to a decision that will be best for everyone involved."

"There is nothing to talk about. I'm done talking. I'll get you a place until you get back on your feet. After the baby is born, I'll pay child support and have custody during the off-season."

"You mean to tell me that I can't live here? Not even sleep in one of the guestrooms?"

"You heard what I said."

"Don't you think it would be best if we were all under the same roof?"

"Didn't I say I'm getting married? What, you think you're supposed to live here with my wife and me? You're crazy!"

"Well, how do you think your little fiancée will feel when you have to tell her your ex will be in labor about the same time you'll be saying 'I do'?"

Massai thought about it and knew instinctively that Alexis would not be happy with the entire situation. "This is a nightmare," he said quietly, holding his head in his hands.

"No, it's not, Massai. This baby is giving us an opportunity to fix what's wrong in our relationship."

"A baby is not crazy glue, Eva."

"But a baby is a new beginning."

His mind flashed back to the three days he and Alexis had spent together. He felt an impulse to call her at that very moment and suggest running away together, elope to an exotic Caribbean island. But he knew that wasn't his reality. He was being forced to deal with what was in front of him, and he was almost certain that as soon as he told her about the baby all the happy moments they had shared would become distant memories.

26

THE DAILY GRIND

In the three weeks since Alexis had agreed to marry Massai, her wedding plans were in full swing. She had already chosen both ceremony and reception sites in New Orleans, and had even booked a caterer who would be preparing Creole-style cuisine for the occasion. Alexis appreciated Massai letting her plan each and every detail. Whenever she sought his opinion his answer was always the same: "What you want is what I want."

Alexis was saddened that Morgan and Claire were not around to help her as the three friends had always planned, but she knew better than anyone that things and people often changed. When she talked to Massai about it, he urged her to call her friends and make up and to explain to them why she was hurt. But her stubborn streak would not allow her to do that.

"What are you doing here?" Alexis exclaimed, running across her half-decorated classroom and into Massai's waiting arms.

She had been back to work for two weeks and she was already feeling fatigued. The principal had a steady stream of new speakers coming in to discuss lesson planning, instruction and classroom management. While

Alexis appreciated their efforts, she often felt as if she was back at Tennessee State University during her undergraduate years. These activities, plus getting her classroom ready, took a toll, and she went home every afternoon feeling as if she had just taught a roomful of overactive children.

"I wasn't expecting you until tomorrow," she said, planting kisses all over his face. Every weekend Massai arrived with a smile, and they would spend his entire stay at her apartment watching movies and making love. The more he visited, the more difficult it became for him to leave. Alexis found herself counting the days between each visit.

"I know, but there is something I wanted to talk to you about, and I really couldn't wait any longer."

Alexis noticed that he was more subdued than usual but told herself he was probably just tired from the plane ride to Detroit.

"Well, if I had known I would have taken off work, or at least asked to leave a little early."

"It's cool, baby. I'll just help you around here until it's time for you to leave."

She kissed him again and then bounced over to her black metal desk. "I want to hear what you have to talk to me about, but first let me show you what I found in this *Martha Stewart Weddings* magazine." Alexis picked up the thick periodical and flipped to the page with a sticky note stuck to it. "Look at this cake, Massai. Isn't it beautiful? I thought we could have something like this, but in our colors."

He looked over her shoulder and sighed.

"What's wrong?" she asked, concerned. She closed the magazine and returned it back to her desk.

"It'll have to wait until we get to your place," he said, looking as if he was in physical pain.

"No, if it's bothering you this much, then we should talk about it now. I'm sure it can't be that bad," she said, kissing him again.

Massai stared at her for the longest time before saying anything. To Alexis it seemed that he was studying her—taking a mental picture and creating a memory. He finally spoke.

"I think we should postpone the wedding." His voice was barely above a whisper.

"Why, Massai?" she asked, her eyes welling with tears before she had the chance to hold them.

"Don't cry."

"Well, I'm upset. Is there something I did?"

"Of course not. I just don't think now is the best time to be planning a wedding."

"You said the sooner the better," Alexis quickly reminded him, wiping away the tears making their way down her cheeks.

"I said that before—"

"Before what?"

"Before I found out that Eva was pregnant."

Alexis had never felt pain so intense. Her mouth moved but no sound came out. Her heart felt as if it had been ripped from her chest and was being stomped on by a giant.

"What?" she asked, hoping and praying that she had misunderstood some part of what he just said.

"Eva is about eleven weeks pregnant."

"And the baby is yours?"

He nodded.

All of a sudden, the tears stopped and she found the strength she desperately needed. How he answered her next question would determine her course of action.

"How long have you known, Massai?"

His mouth opened and closed. He shifted his weight from one foot to the other, finally sitting in one of the student chairs.

"How long, Massai?" Alexis asked again although from analyzing his reaction, she believed she already knew the answer.

"I found out when I got back from Detroit after we decided to get married. She was waiting for me when I got back home."

Her breathing quickened, and though she tried to remain calm, her body began trembling with rage. "You've been here to see me three times since then."

"I know, and every single time I've wanted to tell you, but I didn't know how."

"So you thought the best idea would be for you to wait until the wedding plans were damned near finished and I was at work? You thought this would be the perfect time?" she asked sarcastically.

"No, Alexis, I didn't want to tell you like this."

"I can't believe this is happening," she said, holding her throbbing head in her hands.

"I don't know what to say."

"How about explaining how you could come here weekend after weekend, sleep with me and be completely aware that your ex-girlfriend was lying up in your house pregnant. You didn't say one word, Massai. You just let me walk around as if everything was normal."

"I'm sorry," he pleaded, standing up and walking towards her.

"Stop!" Alexis ordered, holding her hands straight out. "Do not come near me."

"Don't act like that."

"Don't you tell me how to act. You've made a fool of me. Stupid me, sitting up in here picking out cakes and bridesmaids dresses and bragging to my coworkers about how good you are to me. And all the while I'm totally clueless that Eva is in New Orleans picking out cribs and strollers."

"I'm sorry," Massai repeated.

"Hell, yeah, you're sorry. You're a coward, and you *are* sorry!" Alexis saw the pain in Massai's eyes but refused to acknowledge it; his pain could not compare to her own.

"You want to postpone the wedding, but for how long, Massai? As long as it will take for Eva to connive her way back into your bed? I bet she's not even pregnant, but you're just too stupid to realize it. I'm not going to wait for the shit to hit the fan. Forget postponing the wedding. As far as I'm concerned, the shit is cancelled!"

"That's not what I want, Alexis."

Alexis went over to her desk, stacked her wedding magazines and loudly dumped them into the wastebasket. The tears returned, but her intense anger refused to subside.

"I love you, Alexis," he said quietly.

"Oh, yeah, you love me? Well, isn't this a great way to show it? You, on the other hand, make me sick. I hate you."

"You don't mean that."

"Yes, I do. I wish I had never met you. I should have listened to my conscience and stayed away from you in the first place. I knew you would hurt me, and I knew I couldn't take any more pain. You came to my sister's wedding, you met my family and you made me love you. You gave me this." Alexis snatched off the engagement ring in disgust. "You can take this shit back," she said, throwing the ring with all her strength and hitting Massai in the chest.

"No, this is yours. I want you to keep it," he said, picking up the ring from the floor.

"Keep it for what? As a reminder of how you lied to me and strung me along these past few weeks? I don't think so. Why don't you give it to your baby's mama, or better yet, use it for diaper money."

"I don't want what we have to end."

"Well, you should have thought about that before you lied to me."

"Alexis, take the ring."

"Hell, no," she said, slapping his outstretched hand away. "I don't want the ring and I don't want you. Get out of my room and my life."

"I'm not leaving," Massai said stubbornly.

"Oh, yes you are," Alexis said pushing him in his chest with all her might, trying to force him out of the doorway, but he wouldn't budge.

"I want to talk to you about our future," he said calmly.

"There is no future for the two of us. Now get out or I'm going to call school security."

"Fine. Do what you have to do, but I'm not leaving."

She was bluffing; there was no school security. "Okay stay, but you'll be here talking to yourself."

She picked up her bag and stalked from the classroom, leaving him standing alone. Looking straight ahead, she hurried down the long main corridor of the school. Alexis heard the curious whispers and saw the looks from her coworkers but wasn't prepared or inclined to stop and offer any explanation. The tears streaming down her face were none of their business. Never once did she look back and check to see if Massai was coming behind her, even though she desperately wanted to.

27

DESPAIR

"What's going on, Massai?"

"What do you want?" he asked Malik, who was towering over him.

"I want to know why you've been locked in your office watching *In Living Color* reruns for the past week."

"Who told you that?" His voice was unusually raspy and cracked because he hadn't been using it. Malik was the first person he had spoken to—other than Alexis's voicemail service—in seven days.

"Eva told me. She called this morning and said that she couldn't get you to come out of here."

"I'll come out when I'm ready."

"Why are you in here?"

"Because I like it in here; it's quiet. I have a little refrigerator, a bathroom. What else do I need?"

"You need to talk to someone. You know what happened to Tom Hanks in *Castaway*. Have you named your basketball yet?" Malik asked, trying to inject some humor into a very strange situation. "I've never known you to lock yourself in a room for days at a time," he said, sitting down next to Massai on the peanut-butter-colored couch. Malik saw the sparkling engagement ring resting on a brown wooden coaster on the coffee table. He picked it up, bouncing it in his palm. "Isn't this the ring you bought Alexis?"

Massai nodded without looking at him. His eyes were glued to Damon Wayans and David Alan Greir performing a "Men on Film" skit. "She gave it back to me; broke up with me last week." He laughed when Damon Wayans's character awarded three snaps in Z formation to a movie.

"Why would she break up with you? I thought you guys were planning the wedding for New Year's Eve?"

"I told her that we should postpone the wedding, and that Eva is pregnant. She just flipped out and started screaming that we were over."

"So that's why you're in here?"

"I'm in here because if I go out there and see Eva I'm going to hurt her. She's the reason I lost Alexis."

"Is she?" Malik asked.

"Yeah, talking all this pregnancy shit. I think she's trying to run some kind of game on me."

"So you don't think she's really pregnant?"

"You know what, Malik?" he said, for the first time turning away from the fifty-inch flat screen television mounted on the wall of his office. "I really don't know what to think. But I do know that something about her story isn't right, and now Alexis won't even talk to me . . ."

"That may be true, but you can't just lock yourself in your office and act like all this isn't happening."

"When is the last time you worked out?"

Massai, now watching "Fire Marshall Bill", pointed to the corner where a treadmill and weight benches were set up.

"That's great and all, but you need to at least go to your court once a day and do some shooting drills," Malik scolded.

"Don't tell me what I need to do. My game is none of your concern."

"Fine. You're right, but that doesn't change the fact that you still need to get out of this room." Malik stood up and began walking to the door, fully expecting Massai to soon follow.

"Is Eva here?"

"No, she said something about going to a baby store to look at cribs."

Massai frowned slightly but didn't comment. He left his office for the first time in a week, and upon stepping into the sunlit hall, immediately smelled the difference between the stale smelling office and the clean, fresh-smelling main floor.

"So what are your plans?" Malik asked when they reached the kitchen. "How will you find out if the baby is yours or not?"

"I can't until she gets further along. Then she can get an amniocentesis."

"What are you going to do until then?"

"Try to get Alexis back; that's the only thing I can do."

"Don't beg. Women do not want a man who begs. Just tell her how it is and let her decide for herself, and if she still doesn't want to be with you, then it wasn't meant to be."

Alexis rolled over in bed and listened to her phone ring for the fifth time that morning. Even though she had unplugged the phone next to her bed so she couldn't hear it ringing, she had forgotten about the other two in her apartment. Someone was calling every hour on the hour like clockwork, and though she had not checked her voicemail, she was sure the calls were from Massai.

Never in her life had Alexis been so depressed or withdrawn, but with no man and no friends, she had good reason to be. Work was an afterthought as far as she was concerned, and while she was supposed to go in every day this week to finish organizing her room and prepare her lessons for Monday morning, she just couldn't find the strength. She couldn't even remember the last time she had consumed a full meal. For days she had been eating bowls of Frosted Flakes cereal, washed down with jelly jars of red Kool-Aid.

Reaching down, she plugged her bedroom phone back in and pressed the code to listen to her voicemail messages.

"Alexis, this is Claire. I just wanted to call and tell you that I think you are acting ridiculous. Morgan and I are just concerned about what you and Massai are getting ready to do. It's been three weeks; I hope you will call me back. I'm at work."

She pressed seven to delete and felt a twinge of regret. She missed her friends, and it was times like these that she needed them the most. She wanted to call and apologize for the way she had overreacted at the restaurant, but pride wouldn't allow her fingers to dial. How could she call and tell Claire and Morgan that they were right? She had moved too fast with Massai, and now she was paying the price.

"Alexis, this is Massai. I've been calling and leaving messages every day for the past week, but I haven't gotten a response. I need to talk to you. I want us to work this out. Whatever you want me to do, I will do it if it will bring you back into my life. Please call me."

Instead of pressing seven as she normally did after listening to a message, she hit nine, saving his message into her voicemail's memory. Her heart ached for the man she met and fell in love with in New Orleans, but there was no way she could allow herself to call him. She knew that he would just end up making a fool of her again, and she'd had her fill of baby mama drama for a while.

"Alexis, this is Kevin. Give me a call back when you get a chance." His message was simple and to the point.

She thought back to the incident at Seldom Blues. She really wasn't all that surprised when Kevin behaved the way he had. He was the kind of man who made sure you knew who he was and what he was all about. That night, he had made sure that Massai knew that he still wanted Alexis.

Against her better judgment and despite residual feelings of anger towards him, she dialed Kevin's cellphone number from memory.

"Kevin Washington," he answered, sounding rushed and out of breath.

"How are you?" Alexis said, not giving her name. She made sure she dialed star 67 before his number, wanting to make sure he recognized her voice and didn't slip and call her by another woman's name.

"Alexis. You must have gotten my message," he said, passing the test.

"I did, although I'm not exactly sure why you called."

"Just wanted to clear the air between you and me. I think I may have been a little bit rude when you and your friend were having dinner."

"You were more than a little rude, Kevin."

"Blame it on jealousy."

"Don't you mean your male ego?"

"Potato, potata . . ." Kevin laughed. "So how is your boy? Has he calmed down any?"

"I wouldn't know; we're not together anymore," she revealed.

"Oh?" His voice perked up just a little. "I hope your breakup didn't have anything to do with me."

"Don't flatter yourself, Kevin. It just wasn't meant to be, and I think we should leave it at that."

"Okay, I can respect that. So how have you been?"

"Okay, I guess. I fell out with Claire and Morgan, so I haven't been doing much of anything lately."

"So you're just on the outs with everyone?"

"It's not my fault. I think people take me for granted and try to run over me, and then when I put a stop to it, they try to bring me down. I'm tired of middle-school games."

"Let me take you out," he said, cutting to the chase.

"Are you crazy? Didn't I just tell you that I'm not putting up with anyone else's mess? I was including you in that, too."

"I'm talking about going out as friends. Catch a movie or something just to get your mind off your issues."

"Friends?" Alexis asked. She knew better, but in a way going out with Kevin would be a way to get back at Massai, to hurt him as much as he hurt her. And he did have a point, she definitely needed a way to forget about her personal issues, even if it was for just a few hours.

"Yeah, friends. We can drive separate cars, go Dutch, or whatever will make you feel more comfortable."

"I guess there's no harm in that."

"None at all. Let's go see a movie this weekend."

She hesitated and replayed the past few months in her head. Unsettling images of Kevin, Massai, Claire and Morgan all came into her head, causing her to feel both sadness and anger all at the same time.

In the end, she gave Kevin the answer that he was waiting to hear, "All right, a movie, but don't get it twisted; we are not going Dutch."

28

ANONYMOUS

"I can't understand for the life of me why you are buying maternity clothes when you know you'll never wear them," Carlos said, sitting in a chair watching Eva stick a pillow under her shirt and looking at her pretend-pregnant profile in the department-store mirror.

"I know that and you know that, but Massai doesn't. I have to make everything seem normal. If I were really pregnant, I would be buying this store out, and that's what he expects. If I didn't buy any maternity clothes, he would suspect something."

"Eva, this isn't right," Carlos said as she tucked an even bigger pillow under her shirt. "How long are you going to keep this up?"

"As long as it takes. Do you know it's been almost three months since I told Massai that I was pregnant and he is still moping around about losing his precious Alexis?"

"I'm getting sick of this crazy shit, Eva. Look at you. You're jamming pillows under your clothes. I think you're taking this too far. Maybe you should go talk to some-body—a counselor or something."

"What are you talking about? He totally bought the doctor's note, and he's letting me stay there, so I'm well on my way," she said, sounding smugly confident.

"I still don't understand how you got that doctor to sign that pregnancy- verification slip."

She turned around and looked at herself from another angle. "I told you I know the nurse in the office two doors down from where I used to work. We've been cool ever since I came from Chicago. She owed me a favor, and it was time to collect."

"You need to come clean. Stop this crazy shit right now before it ends up really ugly. What are you going to do when he finds out?"

"He won't. I've got everything worked out. In fact, in just a couple of weeks I'll be faking my miscarriage. Can't get too far along, now can I? Then I can return all these clothes and get something in my real size, something fabulous."

Carlos just stared at her. Somehow she looked different to him—selfish and almost insane. Where her hair used to shine and bounce, it now seemed dry and limp. Eyes that used to sparkle now flashed with lies, deceit and schemes. At that moment, he decided it was all or nothing; she would have to stop what she was doing, or they would have to end.

"Eva, look, this has gone far enough. No amount of money in the world is worth all this. How do you even keep your lies straight? I'm beginning to think that you really are crazy, and I'm even crazier for putting up with you."

"I'm not crazy; I'm focused and ambitious, but not crazy. Haven't we been through this before?"

"I want you to stop or we're done."

Eva turned around sharply, letting the pillow fall to the floor. "What did you say?"

"I want you to forget all this pregnancy shit or we're done."

"Are you serious?" she hissed, her eyes narrowing.

He didn't answer. He just looked at her, waiting for a response to his ultimatum.

"Please don't think you can tell me what to do. You do not have that much clout. I really don't need you, and if you leave now, then there will just be more money for me."

"So that's your decision?"

"Yes. I'm not giving this up," she said, bending down to pick up the pillow. "You're not worth it."

Without saying good-bye, Carlos slowly rose from his seat and left. He felt as if a lead weight had been lifted off his chest, and though he knew he would miss the sweet and sexy side of Eva, he could no longer be with someone so evil and malicious. He stepped into the scorching New Orleans sun and thought of Massai and what he must be going through. He was part of the problem, and knew that nothing would be right in his own life until he fixed the situation he helped to create. He then knew exactly what his next move would be.

Two months had passed since Massai had told Alexis that Eva was pregnant, and he hadn't spoken to her since. In the beginning, he would call every day and leave messages, but she would not return his calls. Once she did answer, but upon hearing his voice slammed the phone down so hard it left his eardrums ringing. Lately though, as the NBA's preseason loomed closer and his workload increased, he didn't have the time or the fortitude to keep making these daily calls. He was still in love with Alexis and hadn't lost hope that they would put aside all their issues and get married, but he was beginning to think it was definitely a long shot.

Life with Eva was becoming almost unbearable for him. It made him sick to his stomach to watch her prance around in T-shirts carrying parenting magazines. The happiness he always thought he would experience with a child on the way was not there. All he felt was anger, disappointment and animosity towards Eva for turning his life upside down.

Just a week ago she mentioned wanting to start putting the baby's nursery together. Massai had looked at her as if she was crazy. "Don't you think you should at least be showing before we start setting up a nursery?"

"Some pregnant women don't show until they're well into their sixth month. Do you think I want to be upstairs painting a room and putting together furniture when I'm as big as a house?"

Massai didn't answer and they hadn't talked about it since. But after looking at his online banking statement a few days later and seeing a two-thousand-dollar purchase from an upscale baby store, Massai knew that Eva hadn't listened to a word he said.

Going to the custom-made basketball court made Massai smile. Built in the middle of his home, just behind the main stairway, the court was the only place he really felt comfortable. He walked over to the metal basketball rack, admiring the wonderful job the cleaning crew had done. The turquoise and yellow accents reflected his team colors and the wooden floor proclaimed his jersey number, 26, in the center.

He stood on the free-throw line and bounced the ball twice before shooting. The ball hit the rim, widely missing the hoop. "Figures," he said to no one in particular. "I can't get anything right."

For the better part of an hour, he stood on that line working on his form and accuracy and reviewing his personal life. His life was going in an unwanted and unplanned direction, and he realized he was losing control of his situation. He needed a way to regain focus and a sense of purpose. Massai needed to find a way to prove to Alexis that he was ready to commit to her for an eternity.

Massai had just started running the length of his NBA-regulation court when his cell phone began ringing loudly from the corner of the gym. He considered not answering until Alexis's phone number flashed on the screen in his thoughts. He quickly changed his mind. When he reached the phone, he was disappointed to see that the number was blocked, but it was always possible she simply didn't want him to know the number she was calling from.

"Hello?" he said, exhausted and out of breath.

"Is this Massai Taylor?" a male voice that he didn't recognize asked.

"Yeah, who is this?" he asked, hoping that the caller wasn't some deranged fan.

"An anonymous concerned caller."

"Let me tell you something, man. You don't need to concern yourself about me," he said, getting ready to hang up.

"You should be concerned about what Eva's been telling you."

"Who is this?" he asked, suddenly realizing that the caller was no ordinary fan. This person knew Eva and, because of that association, probably knew him as well.

"I'm the guy who Eva tells all her business to. You don't know me, but I know a hell of a lot about you," the mystery caller said.

"How did you get my number?" he was angry but curious at the same time.

"As I said, I know a lot about you. Your phone number is just the tip of the iceberg."

"That's not answering my question. How did you get my number?"

"Let's just say that I have intimate access to Eva's phone book."

"So what do you want?"

"I just want to let you know that Eva is not who or what she claims to be. I know that she has been telling you she is pregnant, but if I were you, I would get her tested by a doctor of my choosing. You play for the

Hornets; I'm sure you have a team doctor who would do you a favor."

"So you're saying that she isn't pregnant?"

"Oh, it's not like she hasn't tried. She used a sewing needle to poke holes into your rubbers. What I am saying is that she's with you for a lot of reasons, but having a baby purely because she loves you isn't one of them."

"Why are you telling me this?" Massai asked, still trying to place the caller's voice.

"Because I know what kind of woman she really is, and it wouldn't be right if I let this continue without at least giving you a heads-up."

"What's your name?" he asked, already planning to confront her with the information.

The caller hesitated, obviously trying to decide whether or not to reveal his identity. "Carlos." And with that he hung up, leaving Massai to digest what he had just been told.

Massai looked around the gym, expecting Malik to jump out of a dark corner laughing his head off. The phone call had practical joke written all over it. If it wasn't a joke, then something was very wrong. When no one appeared after a couple of minutes, Massai began to think the call may have been serious.

Opening his cellphone, he quickly placed a call to the Hornets' team doctor. The doctor's jovial voice answered after several rings.

"Dr. Warner, this is Massai. How are you?"

"I'm fine. Enjoying this beautiful weather with a game of golf. How about you?"

"Just working out a little bit, trying not to get rusty."

"Good, good. Have to keep that knee strong. You're not having any problems with it, are you?" the doctor asked, referring to an old college injury that bothered him from time to time.

"No, no, my knee is feeling strong. That's not why I called."

"Well, what can I help you with?"

"I feel bad asking you this, but it's kind of necessary," Massai said, embarrassed by his situation. "My ex-girlfriend says she's pregnant, but I really don't know what to believe. I was wondering if we could come by sometime soon so you can give her a blood test?"

"You know, Massai, a few of your teammates have come to me with that same request, so it really isn't that unusual. I'm out of the office today but if you could stop by tomorrow I'll perform the test and get the results for you within an hour."

"That soon, huh?" he said, smiling at the prospect of finally knowing the truth.

"Yes. Normally it takes a couple of days for blood-test results to come back, but we have a lab right in our office so we can get the results back in a matter of minutes, depending on the type of test."

"I really appreciate it, and we will definitely see you tomorrow." Massai hung up, hoping the test results would be his salvation.

29

BABY DADDY

"How are you?" Alexis asked, sliding into the passenger seat next to Kevin. This was their second outing as platonic friends and her thought was so far so good.

"I am fine. How are you?" he said, smiling at her.

"Tired. Exhausted, really. These past few weeks at work have really drained me. I think I could sleep for twenty-four hours and not wake up once."

"Are you sure you're up to going dancing? I can always take a rain check." The new "just friends" Kevin was just as thoughtful as "boyfriend" Kevin was but without wanting something in return. Not once since they had been hanging out together and talking on the phone had he tried anything sexual. She was pleasantly surprised.

"No, I'll be fine. I'm sure I'll wake up once we get there."

"Good, because I didn't want to take you back home, anyway, considering you made me wait over a month to see you again."

"Well, I've been busy. The start of the new school year is always so hectic."

"I'm not complaining. I'll take whatever I can get. You look nice, by the way."

"Thank you. And you look adorably casual yourself," she replied, not used to seeing him in anything other than a suit or boxers. She didn't mean for it to hint of flirting; it just came so naturally. The more time Alexis spent with him, the more she remembered why she had fallen for him almost a year ago. Of course, she could never forget how he had lied to her or the heartache he had caused, but she had forgiven him.

Kevin looked at her, his smile widening. "You're actually looking better than I've ever seen you, and that's a feat in itself. Are you gaining weight or something?"

She glared at him. "What?" she asked loudly. "No, I have not gained any weight!"

"I didn't mean it in a bad way. I was just trying to say that it looks like you've filled out a little. It looks good."

"I wear the same size I have always worn, so you must be imagining things," Alexis said, not revealing that her pants and bras had become a bit more snug recently.

"Okay, okay. I see I've hit a nerve. I just meant that you look beautiful," he said, softening his voice.

They avoided the subject of weight the rest of the way to the community center, where they were going for their first ballroom-dancing class. He had made the suggestion after their movie date, saying that it would be fun, and she agreed.

After their arrival, the ninety minutes went by slowly for Alexis. The community center felt like it was a suffocating inferno. More than once she became so light-headed she had to take a break, forcing Kevin to partner with an older woman whose hands roamed below the belt and whose clothes smelled of cigarette smoke. The full, half and quarter turns the instructor kept calling out made her feel so dizzy and nauseated that at least twice she ran to the bathroom and kneeled in front of the toilet, expecting to lose her breakfast, lunch and last night's dinner.

"I'm so sorry," she apologized, practically collapsing onto the passenger's seat. The two had to the leave dance class early, and now Kevin was driving slowly and cautiously, praying that she wouldn't regurgitate on his leather seats.

"Don't worry about it. Anyway, I was ready to go when that lady I was dancing with touched my butt the first time."

Alexis put her head against the cool glass of the window. "I must be coming down with the flu or something. I feel terrible," she said, clutching her bubbling stomach.

"Dizzy, nauseated and tired . . . maybe you're pregnant." He laughed as if he was at a Chris Rock comedy show.

"Kevin, I don't find anything funny," she said, glaring at him.

"Didn't you tell me that you pulled a baby charm from your sister's wedding cake?"

"I threw that stupid thing away a long time ago."

"That doesn't make it any less true. Maybe the baby's mine," he fantasized.

"Even if I am pregnant, which I'm not, the baby would not be yours. We haven't slept together in almost six months."

"So it's Massai's baby? Somebody you don't even talk to," he said jealously.

"You keep talking about some baby that doesn't even exist. And what are you getting so huffy-puffy about? You have two kids you have to pay child support for already."

"Yeah, but the idea of you having some other man's baby just doesn't sit well with me. Wouldn't we make beautiful kids?"

"You are getting way ahead of yourself. Number one, there is no baby. Number two, there is no way I would ever have your baby. And number three, I am not now, nor have I ever been pregnant."

"So you would have Massai's baby?"

"Are you listening to me? I AM NOT PREGNANT!"

"I think you are."

"What is wrong with you? How many times do I have to say—" Alexis was cut off by the sudden urge to vomit. Breathing deeply, she waited until the feeling passed.

"Alexis, are you okay?" he asked, glancing at her with concern. It was time to face the obvious. All the signs were there, and she knew that she could no longer tell herself that her missing period was due to stress. There wasn't enough stress in the world to make her two months late.

"I'm okay," she whispered.

"We're here," he said, pulling his car into a spot next to hers. "Do you need me to walk you up?"

"No, no, I'll be okay. Probably just caught a bug from one of my students," Alexis said. "I'm going to go get a box of Tylenol PM and then just sleep. I'll be fine. Call me tomorrow."

She got into her car and drove to CVS. Not for Tylenol, but for a pregnancy test.

Alexis's hand trembled as she placed the test stick into the Dixie cup. This was her third attempt to take the test. The first two failed because she was shaking so badly that instead of wetting the test stick, she peed all over her hand.

She held the stick in her right hand and emptied the cup with her left. Less than thirty seconds had passed since she accurately executed the test, but she couldn't wait. She flipped the stick over and felt light-headed again when she saw two clear, solid blue lines. She matched the lines to the picture on the box to confirm that she was indeed pregnant.

"Oh, shit," she said quietly.

She stared at the positive stick and held it until her fingers were numb. Alexis closed her eyes, hoping she would wake up from this nightmare. But this was her reality, and there was no waking up. Alexis thought it was funny how one decision made in a split second could change the rest of one's life.

A baby.

Questions without ready answers popped into her head: How far along was she? Would it be a boy or a girl? Whom would the baby look like? She placed her hand on her stomach and tried to imagine herself with a swollen belly and that radiant, mother-to-be glow.

Many women her age and in her situation would immediately call a clinic to schedule an abortion appointment. No husband and little money spelled the two words Alexis most dreaded: stress and struggle. Although she had vowed never to be in a situation where she would become a baby mama, everything didn't always work out as one hoped and, for Alexis, terminating this pregnancy was not an option.

She felt totally and completely alone. She needed someone to talk to, but looking around her empty apartment she was all too aware that there was no one to confide in.

She picked herself up off the bathroom floor and hurried into the bedroom, telling herself that now was not the time to be stubborn and embarrassed about the predicament she had gotten herself into. She punched in Claire's cellphone number and waited for her oldest friend to answer.

"Oh, my God, I know this isn't Alexis Hunter calling me? Has hell frozen over?" she laughed.

"I'm sorry I haven't called in so long, but I was angry," Alexis said, apologizing immediately.

"Well, I'm sorry that I wasn't a supportive friend. Now is this silly beef over and done with?"

"It should have never started in the first place."

"I totally agree," Claire said. "Now I hope you haven't planned the entire wedding without Morgan and me. I know we had our reservations in the beginning, but we both realized that if Massai makes you happy, then that's all that matters."

"Can you and Morgan swing by here for a little while?" Alexis asked, not wanting to tell them everything that had been going on over the phone. She was on the verge of breaking down.

"I'm supposed to be meeting someone. Remember the little short guy I was with at Alicia's wedding?"

"Claire, it's important. I really need to talk to the two of you." She wiped her tear-filled eyes.

"Are you crying?" Claire asked, her voice slightly panicked. "We'll be there in a half an hour."

"What's going on?" Morgan asked as she and Claire rushed through Alexis's front door.

"I can't believe this is happening," she said, breaking down again.

"Take a deep breath, calm down, stop being so emotional and dramatic and tell us exactly what happened," Claire said, trying to keep her friend composed.

"Massai and I broke up because Eva is pregnant and he didn't tell me until almost a month after he found out and I just took a pregnancy test and now I'm pregnant, too." She blurted out the entire story in one breath, knowing that if she had taken her time she would have never finished.

The room was completely silent. So silent, in fact, that Alexis could hear a piano being played in the apartment downstairs and a couple arguing next door. Normally, hearing a life-changing revelation, Claire and Morgan would have nonstop questions and comments, but this time was different. Both were at a loss for words.

"Did you hear me?" Alexis finally asked, after standing in front of her friends for what seemed like an eternity and getting no response.

"Of course we heard you, but I don't think we believe you," Morgan said, sitting down on the chaise and looking at her friend.

"I would not make up something like this."

"Well, what are you going to do?" Claire asked, also sitting down.

"I don't know. That's why I called the two of you."

"Abortion is out of the question?" Morgan asked, already knowing what her friend's answer would be.

"I'm having the baby," she answered emphatically.

"What does Massai say? What role does he plan on having?"

"I haven't told him yet! That's what I need some advice on. Should I tell him or not?"

"What kind of question is that? Of course you have to tell Massai; he's the father. Are you going to have a child and not tell it who the father is?" Claire asked.

"And what about money? If you don't tell him, he's going to get off without paying a dime in child support," Morgan added.

"Money is not what this is about for me."

"What is it about then? How are you going to take care of this child without some support from its daddy? Its very rich daddy?"

"I'm not sure I want to add any more drama to an already drama-filled situation. I think it would be better to leave Massai, Eva and their baby alone. Let them be a happy family."

"But where does that leave you?" Claire wondered.

"I'll be okay."

"So are you saying that you really aren't going to tell him?" Morgan asked.

"Yes, that's exactly what I saying," Alexis declared. "There is no point in causing more trouble."

"That's crazy. You're being selfish and stubborn, as usual," Claire said sharply.

"I really think you should tell him. For your baby's sake if nothing else," Morgan said, quickly abandoning the idea of millions in child support.

"I don't think so."

"If you don't tell him, I will. I'll call Malik, get his number and tell him. I cannot stand around and let you do something so terrible." Claire meant every word she said.

"You would not do that," Alexis said, looking at her friend in disbelief.

"Oh, yes, I would. What you're trying to do is not fair to anyone involved—the baby, Massai or you. Why don't we say that if you don't tell him by the time you're six months, I can call him?"

"You can't do that, Claire," she said, becoming upset. "Telling Massai is not your place!"

"It may not be my place, but it is in the best interest of my niece or nephew. Now as I said before, tell him or I will."

30

CONFRONTATIONS

Massai waited patiently in the hall just outside his bedroom for Eva to come out. He had asked her out on the pretext of having lunch, but he really intended to take her to Dr. Warner's office. He wasn't sure how Eva would react when he asked her to take a blood test in his presence, but at this point he really didn't care. Today was the day he would find out the truth.

"I'm ready," Eva said, rushing out zipping her purse. "I can't believe you're taking me to lunch, Massai. I mean, it's like you're doing a 180-degree turn. A couple of days ago, you wouldn't even look at me and now you're taking me on a date." Her smile was as wide as a Cheshire cat's.

"I just decided it takes more energy to be angry than it does to be happy. Right now I'm all about making my life easier, and I realized that I could do that by accepting the fact that you're pregnant," he said as they walked down the stairs and out to his Mercedes G Wagon.

"That's what I've been saying all along. I knew you would come around, though." She sat down in the passenger's seat, and Massai closed the door behind her. "So where are we going?" she asked happily, turning on the radio.

"Somewhere new. Someone called me yesterday and recommended this place."

"Oh, okay. I like surprises."

"This is definitely a surprise," he said, driving through the streets of New Orleans.

"I'm just glad that you're starting to think rationally about this whole situation."

Eva continued her chattering on the drive to Dr. Warner's office. The sound of her voice had become like fingernails on a chalkboard, and the more she talked about baby bibs, diapers and bottles, the higher his speedometer rose.

"So I'm assuming that the new leaf you're turning over means that Alexis is no longer a factor in your life?"

He flinched when she uttered his ex-fiancée's name. "What are you talking about?"

"I'm talking about Alexis. You know, the girl you've been crying over these past few months."

"Eva, you've never seen me cry," he said, not appreciating the way she was exaggerating.

"You know what I mean. You didn't cry, but you were pretty upset."

"Finding out you were pregnant and losing Alexis the way I did was difficult," Massai said, parallel parking across the street from the doctor's office. "Anyway, all that's over and done with, and now I'm looking toward the future."

She seemed to have stopped listening to him and was looking out of the passenger-side window. "Massai, I thought you said we were going to lunch?"

"I did, but first we need to run into Dr. Warner's office. He just wants to take a quick look at my knee. It's been bothering me lately."

Eva looked at him skeptically. "I'll wait for you in the car," she said slowly.

"No, no come on. We'll only be a minute, and Dr. Warner would love to meet you."

"Massai . . ." she whined.

"Come on. With you there, I'll be sure to make it quick. I know we've got to get that baby some lunch," he said, laying it on thick.

"Fine, but I do not want to be in here all day."

He breathed a silent sigh of relief when she got out and followed him across the street to the doctor's office.

"How are you, Mr. Taylor?" the receptionist asked. "Dr. Warner is just finishing up with a patient. Go on back to room six, and he'll be with you in a few minutes."

For the first time, he felt nervous about what he was going to do. Being unsure about how Eva would react made him consider that his plan might not go as well as he wanted. He already sensed that she suspected something. On a normal day, there would be nothing that could keep her from introducing herself as his one and only, but now he practically had to drag her into the doctor's office.

"How long is this going to take?" she complained, sitting down in a black visitor's chair as soon as they reached room six.

"Only a second. All he has to do is look at my knee, and then we're leaving for lunch."

"Good afternoon," Dr. Warner said, entering the room and extending his hand to Massai.

"Dr. Warner, thanks so much for fitting me in."

"No problem, no problem," the doctor said, turning to Eva. "So this must be the lovely lady I keep hearing so much about."

Massai forced a smile, "Dr. Warner, this is Eva. Eva, this is Dr. Warner."

He purposely left off the "girlfriend". That was still reserved for Alexis, even though she wouldn't speak to him.

After exchanging pleasantries with Eva, the doctor turned to him. "Shall we get started, then?"

There was a light knock on the door, and a nurse entered without waiting for a response. Eva's expression changed from confusion to horror when she saw the nurse's syringes, vials and latex gloves tucked neatly inside her red carrying case.

"What's going on, Massai? They don't need to take any blood to look at your knee."

"I need you to take a pregnancy test," he said, looking directly into her eyes and trying to read her reaction.

"What?" She chuckled nervously. Eva was never one to make a scene out in public and was doing everything in her power to remain calm, although she was clearly not in control of the situation.

"I want you to take a pregnancy test," he repeated, waiting for the backlash to begin.

"This is ridiculous. I've already taken several pregnancy tests, and they were all positive. You've seen them."

She was beginning to panic, and knew that Massai noticed.

"Look, I'm tired of the games and the lies, Eva. Yesterday I got a phone call from someone named Carlos who said that maybe you're not as pregnant as you claim to be."

"Who the hell is he?" she asked, becoming loud. She couldn't believe Carlos had dropped dime on her, and if it was the last thing she did, she would repay him for his betrayal.

"*You* tell me who Carlos is, Eva. He knew a lot about our relationship, so the two of you must be very close."

"I don't know what you're talking about," she said, playing dumb. "Whoever this Carlos person is, he's probably just jealous of what we have. Let's go home and forget this craziness."

"How can someone you don't know be jealous? You're slipping. I thought you were a better liar than this."

Massai watched her coming apart at the seams, and the more frantic and flustered she became, the more relaxed and calm Massai was. It felt good to know that he was closing in on the truth.

"He's probably some insane fan or something, or maybe a friend of Alexis's. How am I supposed to know?" she hollered, throwing her hands up.

"Why don't Nurse Sims and I step out for a moment? That way, Eva, you can collect yourself and the two of you can discuss this in private," Dr. Warner said, ushering the nurse out. When the heavy wooden door snapped shut, Eva lashed out, her eyes flashing.

"I cannot believe you would embarrass me like that. They're probably in the hallway laughing at me right now."

"Take the test," he said simply.

"Why should I? Because some wacko got your phone number and told you that I'm not pregnant? I don't think so. I don't have anything to prove here. You've seen the test results, and that should be enough."

"Take the test or get the hell out of my life. I will not sit by and let you destroy everything for me, especially if there is no baby."

"Massai, you can't do this to me," she said, not knowing what her next move should be. For the first time since she'd known him, he had the upper hand; this was not something she was prepared for. She only had two options: to take the test or not take the test, and either way the outcome would be the same.

"Take the test."

Eva felt sweat dripping down her arm, and her right leg began to shake. She knew that she was pushed up against the wall and the only thing left to do, the only thing she knew how to do, was to attack.

"I'm not taking this shit, Massai, and you ain't shit for asking me to." She had decided to lay all the cards out on the table. She knew that the relationship she had with him had just come to a screeching halt, but she would not leave being the only one hurt and embarrassed. "So what if I'm not pregnant?" She yelled loud enough for the whole office to hear her. "And thank God I'm not, because the last thing I would want is a baby to take after your weak ass."

He didn't respond; instead, he observed her changing in front of him. She was not the same cool, composed, beautiful woman he thought he knew. She was becoming someone very different right before his eyes; he was finally getting a sense of the real Eva Norris.

"Massai, you are so stupid it makes me sick. I've been playing your ass from day one and you let me. I never loved you and, honestly, I don't really even like you. I used you for what I needed, and now I'm done with you. I was never faithful, and you know what?" she hissed, her face, voice and eyes as wild as an animal's. "Carlos and I have even had sex in your house, in your bed."

Massai resisted the overwhelming urge to wrap his hands around her neck and choke all the oxygen from her body. He felt as stupid and as naive as Eva claimed he was. How could he have been so clueless?

"I hope Alexis never lay eyes on your ass again. I hope you get injured and never play basketball another day in your life. I will make you regret this for the rest of your days."

31

THE REAL YOU

"I'm surprised you called," Kevin said from the couch.

"Why?" Alexis asked, popping in the *Hitch* DVD and then sitting on the opposite end of the plush sofa. They had last seen each other a month ago, after their dance class had gone totally wrong. Since then, she had been to her first prenatal appointment and had even seen the little speck with a beating heart during a sonogram. Although she was becoming more excited about the idea of being a mother, she hadn't told anyone yet. Her family, Kevin and, of course, Massai were all in the dark about the new arrival due in six months. That was the way she intended to keep it, at least for a little while longer.

"Because since you, Claire and Morgan are back to being bosom buddies, I thought you would kick me to the curb."

"Now why would I do that? You have been nothing but a good friend to me, and I really do enjoy hanging out with you. Believe me, we would not be sitting here right now if I didn't." Alexis meant it from the bottom of her heart.

"Yeah, but you know how a woman and her girls are; you and yours are as thick as thieves."

"But there's always room for a lookout," she said, laughing at her own joke.

"If you say so. I don't get the impression that your friends like me all that much."

"Can you really blame them, Kevin? They know all about your wife and kids and how you were less than honest with me. They are my friends and are just trying to protect me."

"Seems to me like they should worry a little less about you and a little more about themselves."

"Well, I think you and I should change the subject before you offend me." Alexis was half-joking and half-serious.

"Okay, okay. I see you're over your little illness. What did you have?" he asked, glad to change the subject, not wanting to upset her by talking negatively about her friends.

"Just a forty-eight-hour stomach flu. How is work going?" She wanted to change the subject again. The last thing she intended to do was discuss her "flu" with him.

"Stressful. With the mayor having a scandal every week, I don't get more than three hours of sleep at a time. Every five minutes it's something else—drugs, prostitutes . . . you know he's not going to be reelected?"

"Well, I think that a lot of it is the media hyping stuff." She paused and looked at the television screen. "I hate to be predictable, but can we change the subject again?"

"Okay, I know what we can talk about," he said, his voice changing as he slid closer to her.

She looked at him strangely. "Do you mind?" she asked, deadly serious. He was invading her personal space.

"Look, Alexis, I think we need to discuss where this is going," he said, taking her hands in his.

When Alexis told Claire and Morgan that she and Kevin had reconciled and were now friends, they looked at her as if she had gone insane. They both predicted that it would only be a matter of time before he made his move, and she was beginning to think that this was that time.

"What are you talking about, Kevin? There is no 'this' to discuss," Alexis retorted, snatching her hands away and moving as far back on the couch as possible.

"I don't want to be just friends. I want what we had before, but I want it to be better."

She laughed out loud. Not only did she find what Kevin had just said to be funny, but her failure to see through his façade once again was laughable as well. It occurred to her that she seriously needed to work on her character-assessment skills. "Are you drunk?" she asked.

"I am completely sober."

"You can't be. Because if you were you would know that there is no way that we can be anything more than friends." Alexis slid off the couch and stood in front of the television set, blocking out Will Smith and Eva Mendes.

"Give me one good reason why we can't be together?" he asked, coming toward her again.

"You want me to limit my reasons to one? Have you forgotten what you did to me? How you deceived me?"

"That was in the past, Alexis, and I've changed since then. I want us to be totally and completely honest with each other. I want us to concentrate on our future together."

"If you're not drunk, then you have been smoking some pretty strong stuff," she suggested, laughing again.

"So this is funny to you? I'm pouring my heart out to you and you're laughing."

"Kevin, you have to admit that this is crazy. We're friends, and that's all."

"Look me in the eyes and tell me that you don't miss us," he challenged her.

She did as he asked and looked him in the eyes. Alexis remembered all the great times they shared as a couple, but those times couldn't compare to the memory of what she and Massai shared in their short time together. He was the man she really missed, the man she really loved.

"Kevin, without even rehashing all the horrible lies you told to keep our relationship afloat, we can never be because I still have feelings for Massai." Admitting out loud that she still felt things for Massai other than hatred not only startled Kevin, but Alexis as well. So telling herself that if she saw him burning on the sidewalk she wouldn't pee on him to extinguish the flames was a lie. She knew that there was no man she would rather be with. "Kevin, I know I probably shouldn't have, but my heart just won't listen to my head."

"So you're going to go back to him? Alexis Hunter is going to settle for being second in command to his baby's mama?" he said, trying to make her see that Massai was not the man she needed.

"That's not what I said. I need to sort through my feelings and depend on myself for a little bit of happiness for a while. But even if I never talk to Massai again, I can tell you one thing for sure, there will never be a 'me and you'."

He stared at her and realized that he was losing to the NBA star again, and he wasn't even in the room.

"Listen, Kevin, if being friends isn't enough for you, then maybe we should just go our separate way—" Alexis was cut off when a set of lips engulfed hers mid-sentence. He grabbed her around her ever-expanding waist and deepened the kiss. She tried to push him away, but his grip and his determination to win her heart were too strong.

She used her freshly manicured nails to claw at his hands, which were fast making their way under her shirt. Desperate and slightly scared, she bit his bottom lip until she tasted blood.

"Damn!" he yelled, staggering backward. He raised his hand to his lips and looked surprised when he saw his own blood on his fingertips.

"I think you better leave," she said, shaking slightly. She was prepared to snatch up the phone and call the police if Kevin took one step in any direction other than the door.

Kevin licked his lips and laughed. "Don't you think you're overreacting just a little?"

"I should have never trusted you in the first place, but I was so desperate for someone to talk to that I overlooked every manipulative and despicable thing you've ever done. This time," Alexis said, walking to the door and opening it for him, "shame on me."

32

WHITE FLAG

Massai guarded his eyes against the sun as he searched for Alexis's car among the cars in her complex's parking lot.

It had taken him nearly two weeks after Eva's confession to decide whether to show up in Detroit and try to convince her to take him back. What other choice did he have? She had not only stopped taking his calls but eventually had changed her phone number as well. Another man would have taken that as a sign that the relationship was over and done with, but he saw it as a challenge. He loved her, probably would all his life, but he wasn't sure if his love was enough. He was scared that too much damage had been done.

Recognizing Alexis's Scion TC, he pulled into an empty spot next to the light- blue car and killed his rental's engine. Since booking the business-class plane ticket to Detroit, he had been practicing what he would say to her. He wanted his words to be air-tight, leaving no room for confusion. He wanted her to know without a doubt that he was willing to do everything in his power to make their relationship work.

Massai felt his phone vibrate in his pocket and slipped it out, saying hello after he recognized Malik's number on the caller ID.

"I don't understand why you keep leaving town without letting anyone know," Malik said.

"I left you a voicemail."

"All that piece of a message said was that you were leaving town for a few days."

"Okay . . ." he said, not understanding the issue.

"I feel like I'm in the twilight zone or something. If my memory serves me correctly we just had this same discussion a few months ago."

"I do remember you saying something similar."

"So you finally decided to fly to Detroit and try to talk to Alexis?"

Massai watched her apartment door and wondered what she was doing inside. "I figured all that going back and forth with myself was just wasting time."

"I am going to assume you have the ring, then?"

"Right here in my pocket. I don't know if I'll give it back to her today. I have to see how things go, and then I can make a decision," he said, squinting his eyes and looking at the door again. This time it opened and a familiar face stepped out onto the landing, licked his lips and straightened his shirt.

"Are you listening to me?" Malik asked, but Massai could only vaguely hear him; his mind was racing.

"I need to hit you back," he said, flipping his phone closed without waiting for a reply from his friend. He watched as the man jogged down the stairs and looked at his rental car with curiosity. Kevin slowed his pace the closer he got to him, and just as he was about to veer in the direction of his own car, the two locked eyes and a look of recognition flickered across his face.

"Well, well, well. What do we have here?" Kevin asked though the drivers- side window of Massai's car.

"What are you doing here?" he stepped out of the car and looked down on Kevin with disgust.

"I think I should be asking you that exact same thing, seeing that you're the one making an impromptu visit to my woman. Not the other way around," Kevin lied.

"Your woman?'

"That's right. See, when you pulled that baby-mama drama and her friends started tripping, I had the only available ear and bed. Life is funny, isn't it? Your screw-up is my gain, so I guess I should be thanking you right now."

Massai stared at him, trying to detect whether or not he was lying. He was getting tired of the drama and sick of people trying to keep him and Alexis apart.

"Excuse me," he said, pushing past Kevin en route to Alexis's apartment.

"I wouldn't go up there if I were you," Kevin said, opening his car door. "Just before we kissed good-bye, she told me how much she still hates you. Do you know she won't let anyone she knows speak your name? She has all your pictures in a box and it is duct-taped shut. Women can be so dramatic sometimes. Don't get your feelings hurt," Kevin finished, hoping that he wouldn't notice the spot where Alexis had bitten his lip. He got into his car and revved the engine. "My advice to you would be to go home and help the little lady plan the baby shower. I've got everything here under control and rest assured," he said, licking his lips one last time, "she's in very good hands."

He drove away, leaving Massai standing halfway between her door and a rental car with an open ticket back to New Orleans. He knew that there was a chance that Kevin was lying, but he considered that chance to be very slim. If he was lying, then what was he doing coming out of Alexis's apartment as if he owned the place?

His heart hurt as he imagined knocking on her door and being told that everything Kevin said was true. He couldn't take being told by the woman he loved that she hated him and had gone back to her ex-boyfriend. The thought of Alexis and Kevin rolling around in the bed and taking post-sex showers in the exact same spot where he had proposed made Massai feel sick to his stomach.

Remembering something she had told him when they first met, he slowly walked back to the car, got inside and started the engine. "Sometimes it's not about giving up, but letting go and moving on for your own good."

It was over.

He needed to move on just as she had. He took one last look at her apartment, put the rental in reverse and left the past to begin his future.

33

DESTRUCTION OF PROPERTY

Eva crossed her legs and hopped up and down. She had been waiting to use the bathroom for the past thirty minutes, and she was becoming desperate. The big bush just outside the hall window was starting to look pretty good to her.

"Would you hurry the hell up?" she called, banging on the door for the fifth or sixth time.

"Don't rush me, Eva! You're in my house and on my time, remember?"

How could she forget? She held up two middle fingers to her friend Tiffany outside the bathroom door but remained silent. As much as she hated to admit it, Tiffany was right. Since Massai had found out that she was lying about the pregnancy, she was forced to stay with Tiffany and her four badass kids by four different but equally deadbeat dads. Sleeping on the grungy, cold floor and waking up with Captain Crunch cereal in her two thousand dollar weave is what her life had sunk to. And on a daily basis, Tiffany reminded her that Carlos was to blame.

She hated him more than she had ever hated anyone in her entire life. When Eva left Dr. Warner's office that day and was forced to catch a taxi to the hellhole Tiffany and her brats called home, she vowed to make Massai pay dearly. But after much thought and careful reflection, and even after he cancelled all her credit cards, sent her car back to the dealership and dumped her clothes on Tiffany's lawn, she knew that her anger was misdirected. After a late-night weed smoking session, Tiffany had helped her come to understand and accept that it was Carlos who had caused her life to crumble.

The bathroom door opened and a freshly bathed and fully made up Tiffany stepped out into the hallway. Nearly pushing her to the floor, Eva hightailed it into the bathroom to relieve herself.

"You know, I got a call yesterday that Carlos was up in The Loft with some hoe?" Tiffany informed her through the crack in the door. She loved drama, and if she wasn't in one herself, causing one was the next best thing.

"Girl, Kay and I drove by his house yesterday with a brick on the passenger's seat. It took all the self-control I had not to throw it through his living room window," she said, washing her hands and joining Tiffany in the hallway.

"That's because you weren't with me. I would have thrown the brick so far through his window . . ."

"That's because you're ghetto."

"No, it's because I am not for anyone disrespecting me and telling my business the way Carlos did you."

"He was trying to play the good guy. He is just pissed off that I chose something over him—even if it didn't turn out like I wanted it to."

"What we need to do is drive by his house and put that brick to good use," Tiffany said, smiling mischievously.

"I don't think so. It's the middle of the day, for God's sake."

"So what? All we have to do is jump in my car, roll down his street and chuck the brick out the window. It's really not that hard."

"You've done this before?" she asked, frowning at Tiffany.

"Once or twice," she answered, attempting to downplay her theatrics. "You'll be surprised what a woman scorned can come up with."

Eva waited by the door while Tiffany told her mother, who doubled as a live-in babysitter, that she would be stepping out for an hour or so.

While driving to the other side of town where Carlos lived, Tiffany constantly tried to engage Eva in conversation about any and every crazy thing she had done to her past lovers. She learned that breaking windows was just the tip of the iceberg. She realized on the way to his neighborhood that her life was becoming exactly what she had feared. With few job prospects and no savings to speak of, Eva knew that she was mere steps away having no place to go. Of course, Tiffany said that she could stay there as long as she needed to, but she was sure that wouldn't last. She would bet that as soon as her friend found a new bed buddy and subsequent new baby-daddy she would be out on the curb faster than the speed of light.

"Isn't this his street?" Tiffany asked, slowly turning past the white neighborhood watch sign and onto Carlos's beautiful, quiet, tree-lined street.

"He lives in the third house from the corner. The yellow one right there," she answered, pointing. Carlos's car was in the driveway, and that made her more nervous. She would have never agreed to do this if she knew he was home. "That's his car right there."

"Ooh . . . Open the glove compartment," Tiffany instructed, parking her car across the street.

Eva opened the glove box and an ice pick fell out. Picking up the weapon, she looked at Tiffany in horror. "I am not about to stab anyone."

"Pull yourself together, Eva. Do you really think I would tell you to stab him? The ice pick is for his tires. Do you know how much it'll cost him to have to replace all four tires?"

Eva held the ice pick in one hand and the brick in the other. As much as she wanted him to pay for what he had done to her, she felt that things were getting a little out of hand.

"What are you waiting for? Slash his tires and then throw the brick. I'll be waiting right here with the engine running."

Eva took a deep breath and got out, putting both items discreetly in her oversized Gucci bag. She jogged across the street looking right and left in case anyone was watching. She stopped in front of Carlos's car and bent down. Taking the ice pick from her purse and taking another deep breath, she looked around one last time before plunging the stainless steel deep into the tire. At that moment, all nervousness left and a feeling of euphoria flowed over her. She hurried from tire to tire, poking deep holes in each one and stopping briefly to listen to the sweet sound of air rushing from the rubber. When she finished, his car sat on flat tires. Tiffany gave her the thumbs-up sign from across the street.

Eva placed the pick back into her bag and removed the heavy brick. She looked around again before holding it above her head. She paused when she thought she saw Carlos walk from the kitchen the bathroom from his large window.

"Hurry up!" Tiffany urged.

She raised her arm up and back, but just as she was about to let the brick fly toward the huge bay window, her heart stopped when she heard the distinct sound of police sirens. She dropped the brick, snatched her purse off the grass and prepared to run as fast as her legs would carry her across the street to safety. But upon turning around, she saw Tiffany put her green Sable into gear and speed away, leaving her standing alone, the evidence in her purse and having no other option but to spend the next few days in jail.

34

DO WHAT'S RIGHT

"Can you see the sex?" she asked anxiously.

The sonogram technician squirted more of the cold blue gel on her protruding stomach. Alexis turned her head and looked at the screen, holding her breath as she waited for an answer.

"Well I can see an ear . . . a foot . . . an arm," the technician said, pausing between each body part to enter data into the computer. "The baby looks healthy and definitely on target with your due date," she said. "She's measuring about four pounds, three ounces."

Alexis rose up a little on the table. "Did you say she?"

The technician moved the wand over her stomach again before answering. "Yup, looks like you're going to be having a little girl soon."

Alexis was ecstatic. Every week or so after she found out she was pregnant, she would dream of a beautiful baby girl who was a perfect blend of Massai and herself. She had held back buying any baby items that were gender-specific. She had a lot of white undershirts and newborn diapers, but nothing else. As hard as it was to wait, she wanted to be sure of the baby's sex before she went crazy in the layette section.

After a few more minutes of pointing and clicking, the technician told her she was all set, and gave her a towel to wipe her stomach clean and a few of the most beautiful, fuzzy pictures she had ever seen.

Alexis drove all the way home with a huge smile on her face. If the technician had told her that the baby was a boy, she was sure she would have been happy, but there was something about knowing that the baby would be a miniature version of herself that made Alexis's eyes fill with excited and joyous tears.

As she pulled into her assigned parking space, her smile quickly faded. In a Ford Explorer parked next to her car sat her sister and mother, and both were waving like maniacs. Alexis wanted to run and hide.

She knew she should be ashamed for withholding news of the pregnancy from her family members, and she was. But she still couldn't bear the thought of disappointing her parents that way.

"Mom, Dad . . . I'm pregnant, but the father is getting ready to have another baby by another woman, so I didn't bother to tell him or you about the one I'm carrying."

The situation sounded completely ridiculous and embarrassing, and no matter how many ways and times she practiced that speech, she still couldn't muster enough courage to actually tell her parents what was going on.

She waved back at her mother and sister and tried to plaster a fake smile on her face. She had been fortunate. Until recently her stomach had shown no signs of the baby growing inside, and this had allowed her to visit with her family without them suspecting a thing. But one morning she woke up with a belly that couldn't be camouflaged by baggy shirts and large winter coats. She hadn't seen her family in a little over a month.

"What are you guys doing here?" she asked, rolling down the car window. She had yet to make any move to get out of the car.

"We came to see you," Alicia said, stating the obvious. "Now get out of that car so we can go upstairs. It's freezing out here." She and her mother got out of the SUV and began walking to Alexis's apartment, unaware that she was not following them.

Dana, Alexis's mother, turned around. "Would you hurry up?"

Looking down at her growing stomach, she knew that it was time to get out and face the music. She grabbed her bag off the floor, took a deep breath and stepped out of the car. She watched as her mother and sister looked at her then whispered something to each other. The looks of shock, surprise and disapproval she had expected to see were nowhere to be found. As she got closer to them, she was better able to read their faces; she saw sympathy and excitement.

"Well," Alexis said, stopping in front of them and waiting to face a verbal firing squad.

"Well, what?" her mother asked, placing her hand on her daughter's belly just as the baby kicked under her blue turtleneck sweater.

"I think you look adorable," Alicia gushed, taking the keys from Alexis's hand and unlocking the door.

"You mean you aren't mad?" she asked as they entered her apartment. She was totally surprised and taken aback.

"About you being pregnant? No. About having to find out from Morgan's grandmother in Kroger? Yes," her mother said, hugging her and rubbing her stomach again.

"How long have you known?" Alexis asked, taking off her coat and throwing it across the back of the couch.

"A little over two months," Alicia answered.

That meant that they knew the last time she had visited.

"Why didn't you tell us, Alexis?" Dana asked, sitting down and looking up at her daughter.

"Because I was embarrassed. I mean, pregnant with no man. Wouldn't you be?"

"I would," Alicia admitted. "Who's the father? Kevin?"

"It's the basketball player, isn't it?" her mother asked.

She nodded, unable to speak.

"I knew it would never work out between you two," Alicia said knowingly.

Dana shot her a look before turning back to Alexis. "So what is he planning on doing about this?"

"He doesn't plan on doing anything because he doesn't know."

"What do you mean he doesn't know?" Alicia asked, confused.

"We broke up before I found out I was pregnant. I never told him. He doesn't know," Alexis explained, trying to simplify a very complicated situation.

"You're crazy," Alicia said disapprovingly.

"You are going to tell him, aren't you?" Dana asked gently.

"Of course I'm going to tell him. If I don't, Claire will, and that'll make everything a whole lot worse."

"When are you going to tell him?" Alicia asked, not believing her sister had gotten herself involved in such a sticky situation.

"I don't have an exact date or time in mind, but soon. Okay, Alicia?"

"Okay." Alicia held up her hands, not wanting to argue.

"I'm having a girl," Alexis announced, breaking the awkward silence that had fallen upon the room.

"Oh, my goodness. We have to go shopping, don't we, Ma? Have you picked out stuff for the nursery yet? The stuff at Pottery Barn Kids is so gorgeous," Alicia rambled on. She couldn't have been more excited if she was pregnant herself.

Dana Hunter stood and walked over to Alexis as Alicia went on and on about wallpaper and bumpers and changing tables. Her mother took her hands and looked deep into her eyes.

"You have to tell him. It's his baby, too, and he has as much right as you do to be involved in this child's life."

"I know, I know. I'm going to tell him. I promise."

"Don't promise me, Alexis. I know who my father is. Promise your daughter."

Massai rolled over in bed and blinked a few times until his eyes focused. He turned his head to the left and looked at the sleeping woman next to him. Flat on her stomach, Kadijah Sinclair breathed in and out so evenly he knew that she was still asleep. Reaching out, he picked up one of her long, soft twists and let if fall from his fingers.

"Good morning," she said without opening her eyes.

"Good morning. I thought you were still asleep," Massai said.

"I'm a very light sleeper."

"How are you feeling this morning?" he asked.

"Peaceful and serene. Your bed is the most comfortable thing in the world." Kadijah finally opened her eyes and smiled at him. Pulling the sheet close to her body she sat up and stretched.

"Are you hungry? I can run somewhere and grab something," he offered. "I really don't have much in the refrigerator right now."

"I would love some coffee. I'm a big coffee person, and if I don't start my day out with at least one cup, I'm off."

"We all have our vices. Let me just jump into the shower, and then I'll go and pick up some coffee and maybe some bagels."

"Thank you," Kadijah called as Massai headed for the shower.

He turned on the water and stepped inside. He had met Kadijah only two days ago, and he wasn't completely sure how he felt about her. She was definitely beautiful, with smooth skin the color of milk chocolate, slanted, almost Asian eyes, and baby-soft twists that reached down to the middle of her back. But he didn't know if that beauty was enough.

Massai had never brought home a woman he met after a game, but for Kadijah and his new-found freedom, he made an exception. She had been waiting at the back exit and next to her was a little boy dressed in a kid's version of Massai's jersey. He wore twists and was the spitting image of his mother.

"Go ahead, Taj; ask Mr. Taylor to sign your jersey." The woman gave the little boy a permanent marker, and Massai signed the jersey while making small talk with the woman he later invited back to his place for a little one-on-one. There was something about her that he didn't want to resist. She was mysterious and intriguing and sexy and he was immediately attracted to her, even though she was much different from the type of women he was used to. When he met Alexis, he knew immediately that she was special and felt the overwhelming urge to get to know her on several different levels. With Kadijah, there was only one thing on his mind when he looked at her: sex.

That first night he found that she liked it rough, with a lot of forceful positions, handcuffs and dirty name-calling. He was more than happy to oblige over and over again. Last night, he used her body as an outlet for all the anger and frustration he had been holding in the past few months. The more he thought about what he had been through and all that he had lost, the harder he pushed his body inside her and the louder she begged for more.

Massai heard the phone ring, but he was already in the shower and didn't want to get out and feel the cold air on his wet skin. "Kadijah, can you answer that for me? It's probably Malik. We're supposed to be riding to practice together. Can you tell him that I'll be ready in about an hour?"

She sat up in bed, reached over and picked up the phone. "Hello?"

There was no immediate response, but she could hear the faintest sound of someone breathing on the other end. "Hello," Kadijah said again, hoping that she hadn't gotten involved with someone who was being stalked. "Hello," she repeated for the last time, about to hang up.

"Um . . . may . . . may I speak to Massai, please?" Alexis stammered. She thought, prayed that she had the wrong number.

"Oh, he's in the shower. Can I take a message?"

Alexis didn't know what to think. Her luck and timing were terminally terrible. It had taken her two days to finally follow through on calling Massai after the conversation with her mother, and now another woman was answering his phone. Somehow she knew that the voice on the line didn't belong to Eva.

"No, no, there's no message," she said, wishing she had never made the phone call in the first place.

"May I ask who is calling?" Kadijah asked, becoming curious about the caller who seemed so nervous and unsure of herself.

"I . . ." Alexis began, stuttering again. "This is . . . can you tell him Alexis called?" She knew that by leaving her name she was giving him an invitation to return her call, but he didn't have her new unlisted phone number, and it would be virtually impossible for him to contact her unless she wanted him to.

Kadijah hung up the phone just as Massai turned the shower off. "Malik didn't give you a hard time, did he?" he asked, coming out of the bathroom with only a gray towel covering him.

"It wasn't Malik."

"Who else would be calling my house this early?" The image of Eva immediately floated through his mind.

Kadijah removed a rubber band from around her wrist and gathered her twists into a ponytail before answering. "It was a woman. She said her name was Alexis."

35

WHAT ARE FRIENDS FOR?

"Why are we painting this room while you're six months pregnant?" Claire asked, wiping her brow.

"Because we have to get it ready. I know you saw all those boxes from Pottery Barn Kids. My mom and dad must have spent a fortune," Alexis said, tying her pink bandana around her head.

Just three days ago she answered the door and found two exhausted-looking UPS men waiting to deliver a baby's crib, dresser, bookshelf and pink and white striped chaise lounge. After the deliverymen left, she received a call from her soft-spoken father congratulating her and saying that he hoped she liked the things he, Dana and Alicia had chosen.

"I'm sorry about my grandmother, but you know how her mouth is," Morgan said apologetically.

"It's fine. I should have told my family months ago," Alexis said.

"You're right. Now all you have to do is tell Massai and you'll be set," Claire said, looking at her friend over her shoulder.

"I called him," she said, rolling a coat of pale pink paint across the wall of what was soon to be the baby's room.

"You called who?" Morgan asked, doubting that she had called Massai to confess.

"You know who. I called Massai to tell him about the baby." She stood back to look at her handiwork. The top half of the room was pink and the bottom half was white, with each color separated by a white wooden divider. Her brother, Aaron, had come in yesterday to paint the ceiling a pale shade of blue with perfectly wistful clouds spread throughout.

"Why didn't you tell us? We could have come over to give you moral support. What did he say?" Claire said, dropping her paint roller in the bucket and sitting down on the plastic drop cloth.

"He didn't say anything because I didn't get a chance to tell him."

"Why not?" Morgan asked, sitting down beside Claire.

"Because when I called some woman answered the phone talking about he was in the shower," Alexis explained, trying to mask the pain she felt.

"Girl, it was probably Eva. Isn't she still living with him?" Morgan wondered.

"I don't know where she's living, but the voice I heard when I called Massai's house definitely did not belong to Eva. I've heard so much of her in the background that I would have recognized her voice immediately."

"So do you think he's seeing someone new?" Claire asked, hoping that wasn't the case.

"I think so. She sounded very after-sex," she said, replaying the short exchange in her head for the millionth time.

"Whether he has a new girlfriend or not, you still have to tell him," Morgan informed her as if she didn't already know.

"I think I should get an extension." Alexis directed her statement at Claire, the person who had given her the ultimatum in the first place. "I think I should get another month to get my thoughts together. This new girl in the mix changes some things."

"Please, you're just coming up with one excuse after another. That chick who answered Massai's phone could have been the damn cleaning lady for all you know," Claire said, standing up and heading for the door.

"It was not the cleaning lady."

"You don't know who it was, and I'm tired of talking about it. I'm going to go get something to eat."

Claire took her friends' orders and hurried out of the apartment. After getting into her car and driving halfway to the fast-food restaurant, she pulled out her cellphone and found Malik's number among her saved contacts.

"How are you?" she asked Malik, knowing that he would immediately recognize her voice. Unbeknownst to her friends, the two talked almost daily, and Malik was still waiting for Claire to take him up on his invitation to visit him in New Orleans.

"I'm good, how are you?" he answered, smiling at the sound of her voice. The more they communicated with each other, the more he realized that he really liked her, but he wasn't sure if it was enough to give up his womanizing ways.

"I'm fine. I saw you play last night," she said, smiling on her end of the line. She didn't know what it was about him, but he did something to her. With just a few words he could always make her feel special. Being the independent woman that she was, she really didn't like the power he was gaining over her.

"So you do watch sports? What did you think?"

"I thought that you shouldn't have missed that layup at the end of the game," she teased.

"Oh, shut up. You don't even know what a layup is," Malik said playfully.

"I know that your team wouldn't have lost if you would have made that shot."

"Did you call me to bash my game, or is there some other purpose?"

"I do have something to tell you, but you have to promise not to be mad that I didn't tell you sooner," she said, taking a deep breath.

"How could I be mad at someone as sweet as you?" he flirted.

"Alexis is pregnant," Claire blurted out before she lost the nerve.

The line was quiet before Malik responded. "So she's going to have that married guy's baby, huh?"

"What married guy? I know you're not talking about Kevin? They were done before she even met Massai," she said, confused.

"Then why did Massai see him leaving her apartment when he was in Detroit? Kevin told him that they were back together," he informed her.

"I can guarantee that they never got back together. They were friends for awhile, but all that stopped when his lying ass practically attacked her."

"Are you sure?" Malik asked.

"Of course I'm sure. Now when was Massai in Detroit?" Claire asked.

"A couple of months ago, after he found out that Eva was lying about being pregnant."

Upon hearing that news, she practically ran into the car in front of her. "Eva was never pregnant?"

"Apparently not."

"Well, Alexis is pregnant. Almost six months, and the baby belongs to your best friend."

"You're lying," Malik said, although he knew she wasn't.

"I don't lie, Malik. I don't need to. She's having a girl, and she's due in three and a half months."

"If she's pregnant, then why doesn't Massai know anything about it?"

"She tried to tell him about a week ago, but when she called, some woman answered the phone talking about he was in the shower."

"Kadijah," he said knowingly.

"I take it by the sound of your voice that Kadijah is not the cleaning lady?"

"She's this new girl Massai has been seeing. I don't think it's anything serious; just a booty call here and there."

"I thought he was so in love with Alexis?" Claire said, wondering if she had made the right decision to call Malik with this information.

"He thought she was doing Kevin! What did you expect him to do?" Malik said in defense of his friend's behavior.

"Why not ask if it was true? What's the point in coming all the way to Detroit without at least setting eyes on her?"

"Look, I'm not Massai and I can't speak for him. All I can say is that he needs to know about what's going on," Malik said with conviction.

"I totally agree with you, and that's why I want you to tell him," she said.

"What! Why do I have to tell him? Alexis should be the one calling, not me!"

"But she won't, Malik. She's dug this hole for herself and she's too scared to climb out. Massai and Alexis have missed enough time together because of lies. I want to see my friend happy," she said sincerely.

"Okay, I'll call him as soon as I can," Malik said, already constructing in his mind exactly how he would break the news to his lifelong friend.

A week had gone by since Alexis had called and Massai still hadn't attempted to contact her. In all honesty, he didn't know if he ever would. He still couldn't get over the fact that Alexis had gone back to Kevin after all he had done to her.

Things between him and Kadijah were becoming more regular. She would come by after games for some freaky sex and breakfast afterward. Massai felt comfortable around her because she never asked any questions about his personal life and didn't press the relationship issue. Kadijah seemed to be content with sex and bagels, and for him that was just fine.

"So what do you like in your omelet?" she asked, opening his refrigerator and bending down to search for eggs and cheese.

He felt his dick grow slightly as he watched Kadijah in her lacy boy shorts and tank top with no bra. "Why don't you handle that omelet later and handle me right now?" he said, smiling at her.

Kadijah left the eggs and cheese on the counter and walked over to Massai. Straddling him, she kissed him deeply and pulled a Trojan from an almost invisible pocket in her red and pink striped underwear.

He heard his phone ring in the distance but didn't reach for it. Instead, he gripped Kadijah's waist tightly and guided her body in slow circular motions on his lap, making him grow several inches in the process. Kadijah removed her tank top while Massai shifted her underwear to the side so he was able to place a finger inside her opening.

He was enjoying looking at and touching her body, but was growing increasingly annoyed by the constant ringing phone. When the automatic voicemail service would pick up, the caller would hang up and call right back. They continued to ignore the phone, which was becoming very hard to do.

Just as the sound of the ringing phone faded into the background, someone began to beat heavily on Massai's front door. Between the shrill ringing phone and the loud banging on the door, he could no longer ignore the fact that someone really wanted, or needed, to talk to him.

"Why don't you get that and I'll finish up that omelet," she said, climbing off him and retrieving her shirt from the tiled kitchen floor.

"I'm going to get rid of whoever this is," he said, jumping off the stool and heading toward the front door. The phone finally stopped ringing, but the banging on the door persisted.

"What do you want?" he yelled, yanking the door open to see Malik standing there holding his cellphone in his hand.

"What the hell have you been doing? I've been calling nonstop for twenty minutes," Malik said. Not waiting for an invitation, he stepped inside the foyer and looked at Massai.

"Kadijah's here," he stated simply.

"Well, I need to talk to you."

"Can't it wait?" he asked, completely annoyed.

"What I have to tell you has waited long enough."

"What are you talking about?" he asked, following Malik into the living room.

"Alexis is pregnant."

Massai looked at his friend with anger in his eyes. "Well, good for her," he said, putting his large hands together to give Alexis and Kevin a round of applause. "Next time you want to tell me that my ex-fiancée is pregnant by someone else, don't beat down my door.

Send an e-mail or something. I hope she and Kevin are very happy together," he said, turning his back on Malik and walking back to the kitchen.

"She's not pregnant by Kevin."

He turned around. "Well, who is she pregnant by if it's not Kevin?" he asked quietly, though he already suspected what the answer might be.

"The baby is yours, man. She's six months pregnant."

"What about Kevin?" Massai sat down on the couch, feeling as if his legs weren't going to hold him.

"There was never an Alexis and Kevin. He lied, and you were too stupid to go up and find out what was going on for yourself."

He shook his head, unable to process what Malik was telling him. "Why didn't she say anything?"

"Are you forgetting about the little situation you had with Eva?" Malik reminded him.

"What should I do?" he asked. The smell of a chicken omelet floated into the living room.

"You need to find a damn plane ticket. Claire is going to hook something up, because there is no way Alexis is going to agree to meet you."

Massai stood up with his heart beating hard and fast against his chest. He thought about the canary diamond in the bottom of his sock drawer, and then he heard Kadijah singing along with the radio in the kitchen.

"What about her?" he asked, nodding in the direction of the kitchen.

"You go upstairs and get your shit together," Malik instructed. "I'll get rid of Kadijah."

36

JUST THE BEGINNING

Alexis dressed slowly for her night out with Claire and Morgan. She was tired. Work for her this week had been the most difficult one yet, and she was seriously thinking about taking her maternity leave early.

Due to her physical exhaustion, she tried several times to back out of meeting her friends at Ristorante Café Cortina for dinner and drinks. Although Italian food was one of her favorites, she really didn't see the point.

"Let's celebrate the end of The Fabulous Three and the beginning of The Fabulous Three and a Half," Claire said earlier that day over the telephone.

"When have we ever called ourselves The Fabulous Three?" she asked, thinking the entire idea was ridiculous.

"Morgan and I do all the time. It's not our fault that you never pay attention."

"Well, who in the hell is the half?" she wanted to know.

"The baby, you dumb ass. Can you please keep up?" Claire said smartly.

"Look, we can do all that celebrating right in my apartment. I should not be forced to drive thirty-five minutes away just to sit up and look at the same people I look at every weekend."

"Yes, you do. It will give you the opportunity to dress up and get all pretty."

"So I'm dressing up to go and drink water?" Alexis asked sarcastically.

"If it will make you feel any better none of us will drink, okay? We can all order Shirley Temples or something," Claire added, trying to appease her friend.

"What would really make me feel better is going straight home after work, getting into bed and sleeping until Monday."

"Well, you can do all that after dinner. Seven o'clock, and don't be late," Claire said, hanging up the phone. Alexis tried for at least three hours to call her back to tell her she wasn't coming, but Claire refused to answer her phone, leaving Alexis without options.

Alexis yawned as she pulled a long, flowing red-and-gold Indian-inspired spaghetti-strapped dress from her closet. She was grateful that she hadn't been forced to buy any maternity clothes; just going up a couple of sizes was a lot easier to handle. Letting her robe drop to the floor, she stepped into the dress and admired herself in the mirror. She slipped on ten gold bangle bracelets, a necklace and gold sandals. A little pressed powder and gloss and she was out the door.

"Are you gone yet?" Claire asked when she answered her cellphone. She had just pulled up to valet parking outside the restaurant.

"I'm right outside. Are you guys already here?" She allowed the valet to take her hand and gently help her out of the car.

"We're not there yet, but we're on our way. Just go ahead and get the table. The reservation is under your name." Claire hung up again, and Alexis made a mental note to go off on her the minute she arrived at the restaurant.

"Ms. Hunter. *Buona sera,* good evening and welcome to Ristorante Cafe Cortina. If you would be so kind as to follow me, we have your table prepared."

Alexis looked around, totally confused and just a little freaked out. She couldn't understand how the hostess knew her name without being told. Nevertheless, she followed her, wanting to get off her feet and order a cold glass of lemonade.

The blonde hostess, who was no more Italian than Alexis, led her through a maze of tables to a section of private tables near a massive fireplace. Several of the tables were already occupied with smiling, whispering couples. She and her girls could become pretty boisterous on their nights out, so Alexis didn't think this particular section would be the best choice.

"This is beautiful and everything, but I'm meeting two *female* friends tonight. I don't think this is the type of atmosphere we're looking for. Do you have any other tables available?"

"Two women?" the hostess asked, looking confused. "I was under the impression you were meeting a gentleman tonight."

"I don't know what would give you that impression. Maybe you got my reservation mixed up with someone else's." Alexis was trying to remain polite, but fatigue was setting in again and all she wanted to do was sit down.

She saw the hostess' expression change from professional to slightly panicked, and the she felt a familiar hand take hers and a voice say simply, "Surprise."

Looking up into Massai's eyes, she snatched her hand away, knowing immediately that she had been set up by Claire and Morgan. "What are you doing here?" she hissed, not wanting to make a scene.

"Alexis, don't you think it's time we talked?" he whispered in her ear before he placed his hand on her stomach.

She closed her eyes and sighed. This was the moment she had been running away from since the day she found out she was pregnant. She allowed herself to be led to the table closest to the huge brick fireplace. He pulled out the chair for her and held her hand as she sat down slowly, moving awkwardly under her added pounds.

He sat down across from Alexis and stared at her. She was more beautiful than he had ever seen her. "You look—"

"Fat?" she attempted to finish his sentence for him.

"Beautiful," he finished for himself.

The two sat for a while, looking at each other and remembering all they shared and all they missed.

"Why didn't you tell me?" Massai asked, breaking the silence.

"Tell you what?"

"About the baby?"

She looked at her stomach and then back at him. "What was there to tell? I'm pregnant and the baby is yours, but I just figured that you would have already got your fill of hearing that," she added bitterly.

"Eva lied. She was never pregnant, despite how hard she tried. I found out that she punched holes into all my condoms trying to keep me away from you." He paused to gauge her reaction. "But it seems that it backfired on her, because you were the one who ended up pregnant." Massai chuckled at the irony of it all.

Alexis was surprised and realized then that she hated Eva, although that hatred wasn't strong enough to make her forget why she'd broken it off with him in the first place. "That still doesn't change the fact that you lied to me for weeks, Massai. You intentionally deceived me. I could have dealt with the fact that Eva was pregnant, we could have worked through that together. But what I can't deal with is lying, not from anyone, but especially not from you." As she spoke, her voice got louder and louder until several couples stopped their conversation to looking at her.

"I didn't tell you because I wanted to try to come up with a solution that wouldn't affect what we had."

"Well, that really worked out well, didn't it?"

Massai didn't answer, but stared at the mother of his child. He hadn't come there to argue. He wanted to be in their lives as more than a part-time father; he wanted Alexis as his wife. "Stop it," he told her seriously.

"Stop what?"

"Stop acting like you don't care. Stop acting like you don't love me."

Alexis decided to come clean, because she obviously was doing a poor job of acting indifferent. "Okay, Massai, fine, I do love you. No, it's more than that; I'm *in love* with you, but I just don't know if I can trust you again. I want *you* to stop acting as if you're not seeing someone right now. I called your house to tell you about the baby and a woman answered the phone. You were obviously not in New Orleans mourning our breakup."

"I only started seeing Kadijah after I came to see you and Kevin came out of your apartment telling me how you two were sleeping together. I thought you had moved on."

"I would have never gotten back together with Kevin on that level. And if you came all the way to Detroit without even talking to me, then you must have wanted to believe him," she challenged defiantly.

"I do acknowledge the fact that the decision to leave without even talking to you wasn't the smartest, but I'm here now to fix it."

"Does your little girlfriend know you're here trying to fix our relationship? Where is she? Waiting back at the hotel?" she asked accusingly.

"She's not my girlfriend. There was only sex between Kadijah and me," he confessed.

"It was just sex? Is that supposed to make me feel better?"

"My heart has always belonged to you."

She felt the baby kicking and squirming under her skin. It was as if she was trying to get her mother to admit that she still wanted to be with him. "She's kicking," she said instead.

Massai stood up and placed his hand over his daughter. His eyes lit up upon feeling movement and he smiled to himself, and then at Alexis. "That's crazy . . . amazing."

"It is," she agreed, wishing he hadn't removed his hand. He returned to his seat and took the engagement ring from his pocket, placing it on the table in front of her.

He sat back in his chair and watched her study the ring. "Where do you want to be?" he asked. "You either want to be with me or you want to be without me. It's that simple. No more games and no more placing blame, because what's done is done."

She felt the baby kick and squirm again, this time even stronger than before. Alexis knew that it was time to stop being scared. Finally, honestly and completely, she decided to take what she wanted. She lifted the ring from the table and placed it on her left ring finger. "Massai, there is nowhere I would rather be than with you."

ABOUT THE AUTHOR

Maryam Diaab was born in Detroit, Michigan, and received a degree in Arts and Sciences from Tennessee State University in Nashville, Tennessee. She currently works as a fifth grade Reading and Language Arts teacher in the Metro-Detroit area where she lives with her husband and two sons. *Where I Want to Be* is her first novel.

2008 Reprint Mass Market Titles

January

Cautious Heart
Cheris F. Hodges
ISBN-13: 978-1-58571-301-1
ISBN-10: 1-58571-301-5
$6.99

Suddenly You
Crystal Hubbard
ISBN-13: 978-1-58571-302-8
ISBN-10: 1-58571-302-3
$6.99

February

Passion
T. T. Henderson
ISBN-13: 978-1-58571-303-5
ISBN-10: 1-58571-303-1
$6.99

Whispers in the Sand
LaFlorya Gauthier
ISBN-13: 978-1-58571-304-2
ISBN-10: 1-58571-304-x
$6.99

March

Life Is Never As It Seems
J. J. Michael
ISBN-13: 978-1-58571-305-9
ISBN-10: 1-58571-305-8
$6.99

Beyond the Rapture
Beverly Clark
ISBN-13: 978-1-58571-306-6
ISBN-10: 1-58571-306-6
$6.99

April

A Heart's Awakening
Veronica Parker
ISBN-13: 978-1-58571-307-3
ISBN-10: 1-58571-307-4
$6.99

Breeze
Robin Lynette Hampton
ISBN-13: 978-1-58571-308-0
ISBN-10: 1-58571-308-2
$6.99

May

I'll Be Your Shelter
Giselle Carmichael
ISBN-13: 978-1-58571-309-7
ISBN-10: 1-58571-309-0
$6.99

Careless Whispers
Rochelle Alers
ISBN-13: 978-1-58571-310-3
ISBN-10: 1-58571-310-4
$6.99

June

Sin
Crystal Rhodes
ISBN-13: 978-1-58571-311-0
ISBN-10: 1-58571-311-2
$6.99

Dark Storm Rising
Chinelu Moore
ISBN-13: 978-1-58571-312-7
ISBN-10: 1-58571-312-0
$6.99

2008 Reprint Mass Market Titles (continued)

July

Object of His Desire
A.C. Arthur
ISBN-13: 978-1-58571-313-4
ISBN-10: 1-58571-313-9
$6.99

Angel's Paradise
Janice Angelique
ISBN-13: 978-1-58571-314-1
ISBN-10: 1-58571-314-7
$6.99

August

Unbreak My Heart
Dar Tomlinson
ISBN-13: 978-1-58571-315-8
ISBN-10: 1-58571-315-5
$6.99

All I Ask
Barbara Keaton
ISBN-13: 978-1-58571-316-5
ISBN-10: 1-58571-316-3
$6.99

September

Icie
Pamela Leigh Starr
ISBN-13: 978-1-58571-275-5
ISBN-10: 1-58571-275-2
$6.99

At Last
Lisa Riley
ISBN-13: 978-1-58571-276-2
ISBN-10: 1-58571-276-0
$6.99

October

Everlastin' Love
Gay G. Gunn
ISBN-13: 978-1-58571-277-9
ISBN-10: 1-58571-277-9
$6.99

Three Wishes
Seressia Glass
ISBN-13: 978-1-58571-278-6
ISBN-10: 1-58571-278-7
$6.99

November

Yesterday Is Gone
Beverly Clark
ISBN-13: 978-1-58571-279-3
ISBN-10: 1-58571-279-5
$6.99

Again My Love
Kayla Perrin
ISBN-13: 978-1-58571-280-9
ISBN-10: 1-58571-280-9
$6.99

December

Office Policy
A.C. Arthur
ISBN-13: 978-1-58571-281-6
ISBN-10: 1-58571-281-7
$6.99

Rendezvous With Fate
Jeanne Sumerix
ISBN-13: 978-1-58571-283-3
ISBN-10: 1-58571-283-3
$6.99

2008 New Mass Market Titles

January

Where I Want To Be
Maryam Diaab
ISBN-13: 978-1-58571-268-7
ISBN-10: 1-58571-268-X
$6.99

Never Say Never
Michele Cameron
ISBN-13: 978-1-58571-269-4
ISBN-10: 1-58571-269-8
$6.99

February

Stolen Memories
Michele Sudler
ISBN-13: 978-1-58571-270-0
ISBN-10: 1-58571-270-1
$6.99

Dawn's Harbor
Kymberly Hunt
ISBN-13: 978-1-58571-271-7
ISBN-10: 1-58571-271-X
$6.99

March

Undying Love
Renee Alexis
ISBN-13: 978-1-58571-272-4
ISBN-10: 1-58571-272-8
$6.99

Blame It On Paradise
Crystal Hubbard
ISBN-13: 978-1-58571-273-1
ISBN-10: 1-58571-273-6
$6.99

April

When A Man Loves A Woman
La Connie Taylor-Jones
ISBN-13: 978-1-58571-274-8
ISBN-10: 1-58571-274-4
$6.99

Choices
Tammy Williams
ISBN-13: 978-1-58571-300-4
ISBN-10: 1-58571-300-7
$6.99

May

Dream Runner
Gail McFarland
ISBN-13: 978-1-58571-317-2
ISBN-10: 1-58571-317-1
$6.99

Southern Fried Standards
S.R. Maddox
ISBN-13: 978-1-58571-318-9
ISBN-10: 1-58571-318-X
$6.99

June

Looking for Lily
Africa Fine
ISBN-13: 978-1-58571-319-6
ISBN-10: 1-58571-319-8
$6.99

Bliss, Inc.
Chamein Canton
ISBN-13: 978-1-58571-325-7
ISBN-10: 1-58571-325-2
$6.99

2008 New Mass Market Titles (continued)

July

Love's Secrets
Yolanda McVey
ISBN-13: 978-1-58571-321-9
ISBN-10: 1-58571-321-X
$6.99

Things Forbidden
Maryam Diaab
ISBN-13: 978-1-58571-327-1
ISBN-10: 1-58571-327-9
$6.99

August

Storm
Pamela Leigh Starr
ISBN-13: 978-1-58571-323-3
ISBN-10: 1-58571-323-6
$6.99

Passion's Furies
AlTonya Washington
ISBN-13: 978-1-58571-324-0
ISBN-10: 1-58571-324-4
$6.99

September

Mr Fix-It
Crystal Hubbard
ISBN-13: 978-1-58571-326-4
ISBN-10: 1-58571-326-0
6.99

October

November

December

The More Things Change
Chamein Canton
ISBN-13: 978-1-58571-328-8
ISBN-10: 1-58571-328-7
6.99

Other Genesis Press, Inc. Titles

A Dangerous Deception	J.M. Jeffries	$8.95
A Dangerous Love	J.M. Jeffries	$8.95
A Dangerous Obsession	J.M. Jeffries	$8.95
A Dangerous Woman	J.M. Jeffries	$9.95
A Dead Man Speaks	Lisa Jones Johnson	$12.95
A Drummer's Beat to Mend	Kei Swanson	$9.95
A Happy Life	Charlotte Harris	$9.95
A Heart's Awakening	Veronica Parker	$9.95
A Lark on the Wing	Phyliss Hamilton	$9.95
A Love of Her Own	Cheris F. Hodges	$9.95
A Love to Cherish	Beverly Clark	$8.95
A Lover's Legacy	Veronica Parker	$9.95
A Pefect Place to Pray	I.L. Goodwin	$12.95
A Risk of Rain	Dar Tomlinson	$8.95
A Twist of Fate	Beverly Clark	$8.95
A Will to Love	Angie Daniels	$9.95
Acquisitions	Kimberley White	$8.95
Across	Carol Payne	$12.95
After the Vows	Leslie Esdaile	$10.95
(Summer Anthology)	T.T. Henderson	
	Jacqueline Thomas	
Again My Love	Kayla Perrin	$10.95
Against the Wind	Gwynne Forster	$8.95
All I Ask	Barbara Keaton	$8.95
Ambrosia	T.T. Henderson	$8.95
An Unfinished Love Affair	Barbara Keaton	$8.95
And Then Came You	Dorothy Elizabeth Love	$8.95
Angel's Paradise	Janice Angelique	$9.95
At Last	Lisa G. Riley	$8.95
Best of Friends	Natalie Dunbar	$8.95
Between Tears	Pamela Ridley	$12.95
Beyond the Rapture	Beverly Clark	$9.95
Blaze	Barbara Keaton	$9.95

Other Genesis Press, Inc. Titles (continued)

Other Genesis Press, Inc. Titles (continued)

Indigo After Dark Vol. II	Dolores Bundy/Cole Riley	$10.95
Indigo After Dark Vol. III	Montana Blue/Coco Morena	$10.95
Indigo After Dark Vol. IV	Cassandra Colt/	$14.95
	Diana Richeaux	
Indigo After Dark Vol. V	Delilah Dawson	$14.95
Icie	Pamela Leigh Starr	$8.95
I'll Be Your Shelter	Giselle Carmichael	$8.95
I'll Paint a Sun	A.J. Garrotto	$9.95
Illusions	Pamela Leigh Starr	$8.95
Indiscretions	Donna Hill	$8.95
Intentional Mistakes	Michele Sudler	$9.95
Interlude	Donna Hill	$8.95
Intimate Intentions	Angie Daniels	$8.95
Ironic	Pamela Leigh Starr	$9.95
Jolie's Surrender	Edwina Martin-Arnold	$8.95
Kiss or Keep	Debra Phillips	$8.95
Lace	Giselle Carmichael	$9.95
Last Train to Memphis	Elsa Cook	$12.95
Lasting Valor	Ken Olsen	$24.95
Let's Get It On	Dyanne Davis	$9.95
Let Us Prey	Hunter Lundy	$25.95
Life Is Never As It Seems	J.J. Michael	$12.95
Lighter Shade of Brown	Vicki Andrews	$8.95
Love Always	Mildred E. Riley	$10.95
Love Doesn't Come Easy	Charlyne Dickerson	$8.95
Love in High Gear	Charlotte Roy	$9.95
Love Lasts Forever	Dominiqua Douglas	$9.95
Love Me Carefully	A.C. Arthur	$9.95
Love Unveiled	Gloria Greene	$10.95
Love's Deception	Charlene Berry	$10.95
Love's Destiny	M. Loui Quezada	$8.95
Mae's Promise	Melody Walcott	$8.95
Magnolia Sunset	Giselle Carmichael	$8.95

Other Genesis Press, Inc. Titles (continued)

Matters of Life and Death	Lesego Malepe, Ph.D.	$15.95
Meant to Be	Jeanne Sumerix	$8.95
Midnight Clear	Leslie Esdaile	$10.95
(Anthology)	Gwynne Forster	
	Carmen Green	
	Monica Jackson	
Midnight Magic	Gwynne Forster	$8.95
Midnight Peril	Vicki Andrews	$10.95
Misconceptions	Pamela Leigh Starr	$9.95
Misty Blue	Dyanne Davis	$9.95
Montgomery's Children	Richard Perry	$14.95
My Buffalo Soldier	Barbara B. K. Reeves	$8.95
Naked Soul	Gwynne Forster	$8.95
Next to Last Chance	Louisa Dixon	$24.95
Nights Over Egypt	Barbara Keaton	$9.95
No Apologies	Seressia Glass	$8.95
No Commitment Required	Seressia Glass	$8.95
No Ordinary Love	Angela Weaver	$9.95
No Regrets	Mildred E. Riley	$8.95
Notes When Summer Ends	Beverly Lauderdale	$12.95
Nowhere to Run	Gay G. Gunn	$10.95
O Bed! O Breakfast!	Rob Kuehnle	$14.95
Object of His Desire	A. C. Arthur	$8.95
Office Policy	A. C. Arthur	$9.95
Once in a Blue Moon	Dorianne Cole	$9.95
One Day at a Time	Bella McFarland	$8.95
Only You	Crystal Hubbard	$9.95
Outside Chance	Louisa Dixon	$24.95
Passion	T.T. Henderson	$10.95
Passion's Blood	Cherif Fortin	$22.95
Passion's Journey	Wanda Thomas	$8.95
Past Promises	Jahmel West	$8.95
Path of Fire	T.T. Henderson	$8.95

Other Genesis Press, Inc. Titles (continued)

Other Genesis Press, Inc. Titles (continued)

Someone to Love	Alicia Wiggins	$8.95
Song in the Park	Martin Brant	$15.95
Soul Eyes	Wayne L. Wilson	$12.95
Soul to Soul	Donna Hill	$8.95
Southern Comfort	J.M. Jeffries	$8.95
Still the Storm	Sharon Robinson	$8.95
Still Waters Run Deep	Leslie Esdaile	$8.95
Stories to Excite You	Anna Forrest/Divine	$14.95
Subtle Secrets	Wanda Y. Thomas	$8.95
Suddenly You	Crystal Hubbard	$9.95
Sweet Repercussions	Kimberley White	$9.95
Sweet Tomorrows	Kimberly White	$8.95
Taken by You	Dorothy Elizabeth Love	$9.95
Tattooed Tears	T. T. Henderson	$8.95
The Color Line	Lizzette Grayson Carter	$9.95
The Color of Trouble	Dyanne Davis	$8.95
The Disappearance of Allison Jones	Kayla Perrin	$5.95
The Honey Dipper's Legacy	Pannell-Allen	$14.95
The Joker's Love Tune	Sidney Rickman	$15.95
The Little Pretender	Barbara Cartland	$10.95
The Love We Had	Natalie Dunbar	$8.95
The Man Who Could Fly	Bob & Milana Beamon	$18.95
The Missing Link	Charlyne Dickerson	$8.95
The Price of Love	Sinclair LeBeau	$8.95
The Smoking Life	Ilene Barth	$29.95
The Words of the Pitcher	Kei Swanson	$8.95
Three Wishes	Seressia Glass	$8.95
Through the Fire	Seressia Glass	$9.95
Ties That Bind	Kathleen Suzanne	$8.95
Tiger Woods	Libby Hughes	$5.95
Time is of the Essence	Angie Daniels	$9.95
Timeless Devotion	Bella McFarland	$9.95
Tomorrow's Promise	Leslie Esdaile	$8.95

WHERE I WANT TO BE

Truly Inseparable	Wanda Y. Thomas	$8.95
Unbreak My Heart	Dar Tomlinson	$8.95
Uncommon Prayer	Kenneth Swanson	$9.95
Unconditional	A.C. Arthur	$9.95
Unconditional Love	Alicia Wiggins	$8.95
Under the Cherry Moon	Christal Jordan-Mims	$12.95
Unearthing Passions	Elaine Sims	$9.95
Until Death Do Us Part	Susan Paul	$8.95
Vows of Passion	Bella McFarland	$9.95
Wedding Gown	Dyanne Davis	$8.95
What's Under Benjamin's Bed	Sandra Schaffer	$8.95
When Dreams Float	Dorothy Elizabeth Love	$8.95
Whispers in the Night	Dorothy Elizabeth Love	$8.95
Whispers in the Sand	LaFlorya Gauthier	$10.95
Wild Ravens	Altonya Washington	$9.95
Yesterday Is Gone	Beverly Clark	$10.95
Yesterday's Dreams, Tomorrow's Promises	Reon Laudat	$8.95
Your Precious Love	Sinclair LeBeau	$8.95

ESCAPE WITH INDIGO !!!!

Join Indigo Book Club©
It's simple, easy and secure.

Sign up and receive the new releases
every month + Free shipping and
20% off the cover price.

Go online to www.genesis-press.com
and click on Bookclub or
call 1-888-INDIGO-1

Order Form

Mail to: Genesis Press, Inc.
P.O. Box 101
Columbus, MS 39703

Name _____

Address _____

City/State _____ Zip _____

Telephone _____

Ship to (if different from above)

Name _____

Address _____

City/State _____ Zip _____

Telephone _____

Credit Card Information

Credit Card # _____ ☐ Visa ☐ Mastercard

Expiration Date (mm/yy) _____ ☐ AmEx ☐ Discover

Qty.	Author	Title	Price	Total

Use this order

form, or call

1-888-INDIGO-1

Total for books _____

Shipping and handling:
  $5 first two books,
  $1 each additional book _____

Total S & H _____

Total amount enclosed _____

Mississippi residents add 7% sales tax